11-20

HOT LEAD, COLD JUSTICE

HOT LEAD, COLD JUSTICE

MICKEY SPILLANE
AND MAX ALLAN COLLINS

THORNDIKE PRESS
A part of Gale, a Cengage Company

GALE
A Cengage Company

Copyright © 2019 by Mickey Spillane Publishing, LLC.
A Caleb York Western.
Thorndike Press, a part of Gale, a Cengage Company.

LIBRARY OF CONGRESS CIP DATA ON FILE.
CATALOGUING IN PUBLICATION FOR THIS BOOK
IS AVAILABLE FROM THE LIBRARY OF CONGRESS

ISBN-13: 978-1-4328-7786-6 (hardcover alk. paper)

Published in 2020 by arrangement with Kensington Books, an imprint of Kensington Publishing Corp.

Printed in Mexico
Print Number: 01   Print Year: 2020

In memory of
JEB ROSEBROOK,
creator of *Junior Bonner*
and a genuine Western hero

Courage is being scared to death
but saddling up anyway.

— John Wayne

MICKEY SPILLANE
AND CALEB YORK:
AN INTRODUCTION

For many readers over the age of forty or so, the name Mickey Spillane is almost certainly a familiar one. Baby boomers like myself grew up knowing Spillane as one of the most famous writers of the day, and the best-selling (and most controversial) American mystery writer of all.

Other readers will likely remember Mickey as the star of a popular and very funny series of Miller Lite beer commercials running from 1973 through 1988 (co-starring Lee Meredith of *Producers* fame as "the Doll"). And Mickey's iconic private eye Mike Hammer was memorably portrayed by actor Stacy Keach in various TV series and TV movies as late as 1998.

I began writing these introductions to the new Caleb York Westerns to share the background of Mickey's friendship with screen legend John Wayne, and how it led to a screenplay for the Duke that was never produced, but decades later led to a series of successful novels.

It occurs to me that some younger readers, however, may not be familiar with this last of the major mystery writers of the twentieth century, who "left the building" in July 2006. This is despite the fact that only a handful of writers in the genre — Agatha Christie, Dashiell Hammett, and Raymond Chandler among them — ever achieved such superstar status.

Spillane's position is unique — reviled by many mainstream critics, despised and envied by a number of his contemporaries in the very field he revitalized, the creator of Mike Hammer has had an impact not just on mystery and suspense fiction but popular culture in general.

The success of the reprint editions of his startlingly violent and sexy novels jump-started the paperback original, and his redefinition of the action hero as a tough guy who mercilessly executes villains and who sleeps with beautiful, willing women remains influential to this day (*Sin City* is graphic novelist Frank Miller's homage).

This was something entirely new in mystery fiction, which got him called a fascist by left-leaning critics and a libertine by right-leaning ones. In between were millions of readers who turned Spillane's first six Hammer novels into the best-selling private eye novels of all time.

As success raged around him, Mickey Spillane proved himself a showman and a marketing genius; he became as famous as his creation, appearing on book jackets with gun in hand and fedora on head. His image became synonymous with Hammer's, more so even than any of the actors who portrayed the private eye (for the late 1950s *Mickey Spillane's Mike Hammer* TV series, Darren McGavin was said to have been cast, in part, because of his physical resemblance to the detective's creator).

And, ultimately, Mickey himself appeared as his own famous character in the 1963 film *The Girl Hunters.* Critics at the time viewed his performance favorably, and today many viewers of the quirky, made-in-England film still do.

Of course, *The Girl Hunters* wasn't Spillane's first feature film — it wasn't even his first leading role in one. In 1954, John Wayne hired Spillane to star with Pat O'Brien and lion-tamer Clyde Beatty in *Ring of Fear,* a film Spillane co-scripted without credit, receiving a white Jaguar as a gift from producer Wayne (the attached card read, "Thanks — Duke").

11

Mike Hammer paved the way for James Bond — *Casino Royale* is a British variation on Spillane, right down to its last line — and every tough action hero who followed, whether P.I. or cop, lone avenger or government agent, from Shaft to Billy Jack, from Dirty Harry to Jack Bauer. The latest Hammer-style heroes include an unlikely one — the vengeance-driven young woman of the Lisabeth Salander novels — as well as a perhaps more obvious descendent, Lee Child's Jack Reacher.

I was lucky enough to know Mickey Spillane and work with him, and was asked by him shortly before his death to complete a number of his unfinished novels, manuscripts covering the entire span of the writer's career. Thus far I have completed thirteen novels begun by Mickey, ten featuring Mike Hammer, as well as numerous short stories, again working from material Mickey began.

My friendship with Mickey centered on more than my admiration for him and his work — I became one of the few fellow writers in his life. He had many friends in South Carolina, where he lived for decades, and they ranged from auto mechanics to dentists, handymen to lawyers. But after the passing of his writer pal Dave Gerrity, I became — on my numerous visits — someone he could talk with about the craft, and business, of writing.

Early on it became clear that Mickey's few regrets included not working more in the Western genre. He shared stories about John Wayne and dug out the screenplay about Caleb York for me to read. He talked about the TV series *Have Gun — Will Travel,* the creation of which he said he had a hand in, though he never took any credit (or, for that matter, legal action). I have no proof to back him up, although I know he was a friend and collaborator of *Star Trek* creator Gene Roddenberry, who worked on *Have Gun.*

In the weeks before his death, Mickey said to his wife Jane, "Give everything to Max — he'll know what to do," referring to his voluminous files of incomplete manuscripts and story ideas. For over a decade, Jane and I have worked diligently to do Mickey's bidding, and part of that effort has been to see one of his pet projects — Caleb York — brought to light.

This is the fifth Caleb York novel. The first, *The Legend of Caleb York,* was directly based on Mickey's screenplay for John Wayne. For the books that have followed, I have drawn from various drafts of that screenplay and notes in the Spillane files.

13

As I have mentioned previously, John Wayne's interest in "The Saga of Cali York" (as it was originally called — I dropped the "Cali" nickname) does not mean that Wayne necessarily intended to play York himself. He might have — it was written around the time when the Duke was playing roles of a similar nature. Caleb York could easily slip into the world of *The Searchers* or *Rio Bravo,* for example.

But Wayne was also a producer, through his Batjac production company, and might well have cast another star of his day as York — after all, he used Randolph Scott, Glenn Ford, Robert Mitchum, James Arness (his discovery), Kirk Douglas, and even Victor Mature in various Western films he produced.

So for *Hot Lead, Cold Justice* I once again encourage you to cast the York part in any way you like — not that Wayne himself is a bad choice at all.

— Max Allan Collins

CHAPTER ONE

Far north of New Mexico — in the territories of Montana, Wyoming, and the black hills of Dakota — the snow started in November, light and cooling after a blazing hell of a summer. But as that snow fell harder and gathered itself deeper, and the temperature dropped to fifty below, livestock was soon starving in the whiplash wind. What stubby, scant grass there was lay hidden beneath drifting snow that would thaw only to freeze and then provide a platform for more snow to pile onto.

And in early January, when snowfall became a blizzard, the white stuff coating plateaus and filling river bottoms, the cattle began to starve and die by the thousands as their owners — who had not stored away nearly enough hay for such circumstances — stood defenseless against a winter worse than the blazing summer they'd just somehow survived. No spring roundup this year — not after this big die-up, as some wag lost to history put it. But in

Trinidad, New Mexico, that killing blizzard the ranchers and town folk were hearing about was a world away, up north. Surely the conflagration of white would never reach as far as their Territory, much less Texas beyond.

Jonathan P. Tulley, the first snowflakes kissing his grizzled face, paused to stick his tongue out to taste a few.

At a little after ten p.m., the old desert rat turned deputy — a transition that had included Tulley's status as town drunk and resident character — was just starting his nightly rounds. As it happened, the stretch of boardwalk down which he patrolled right now was where he once had tucked himself under and away each night. His former home, you might say.

Now he lived in the adobe-walled jail, sleeping in a cell. Incarceration might well seem a questionable step up, but unlike the prisoners — of which currently there were none — his quarters went unlocked. Since he worked a good share of the night, finding lodgings elsewhere had not been high on his list. Anyway, he preferred the comfy cot of his cell to the stall at the livery stable where for a time he'd worked and slept. That was before Caleb York had come to town, not yet a year ago, and changed everything around for Jonathan P. Tulley.

No more did the bony, bandy-legged figure wear a frayed BVD shirt and baggy, high-water, canvas trousers. Now, at Sheriff York's prodding, Tulley was strictly store-bought attired, from his dark flannel shirt to his gray woolen pants, sporting crisp red suspenders and work boots with nary a speck of horse manure top nor bottom. Once a month the town barber (who was also the town mayor) spruced the deputy up, trimming Tulley's white, wispy hair and combing over the bald spot, the deputy's beard full but not so damn bushy no more. The only remnant of his prior wardrobe was a shapeless canvas thing that claimed to be a hat.

He began his rounds with the little barrio across from the sheriff's office with jail. The low-riding adobe buildings were mostly quiet in the gentle but steady snowfall, hardly a light burning, with the exception of the always lively Cantina de Toro Rojo at the dead end of the shabby smattering of dwellings. He didn't bother going into the cantina, just peeked in the windows.

The fat owner, also his own bartender, was polishing unwashed glasses behind the counter while the usual hombre seated in one corner was smoking a cigarette of his own making and playing fancy guitar while a girl twirly danced and tried to attract customers. She was one of the fallen angels who worked on the second floor of the two-story cantina. Now that the Victory Saloon had shut down its brothel business, this was the only place you could buy a little love in Trinidad. The señorita wasn't getting any real interest from the mix of town people and cowboys mingling with a few local Mexicanos.

That's how cold and quiet this night was.

As he walked along, checking the doors of Trinidad's various storefronts (Harris Mercantile, Davis Apothecary, Mathers and Sons Hardware), with all but the Victory Saloon closed for business at this hour, Tulley was thinking how it was too bad this snowfall, light as it was, hadn't arrived in time for an old-fashioned Christmas. How nice that would've been for the kiddies, toy soldiers for the boys and pretty dollies for the girls, a tree inside with glass ornaments and tiny candles burning.

Years ago, before his wife died of the yellow fever, when he hadn't yet left his now motherless daughter with her aunt and lit out, looking for gold and silver that he never quite found, Jonathan P. Tulley had lived a normal life that included such things as Christmas, right down to a little pine tree taken indoors and all decked out. Where he once lived, there'd been Yuletide snow, too. Now there was snow, some anyway, but Christmas was over and gone.

Not that Christmas had missed Trinidad entirely. There'd been doings at Missionary Baptist and at the Victory Saloon, too (rather different in nature). Some red ribbons and bunting got strung up along Main Street. But lots of folks went by wagon over to Las Vegas, the biggest little town in this part of New Mexico, for celebrating, whether the family variety or the whooping it up kind.

Next year might be different. By this time next calendar, the Santa Fe Railroad spur would have likely got itself finished up, linking Trinidad to Las Vegas. Trinidad would have grown some by then. Several new businesses were already in — most recent, Maxwell Boots, Saddle, and Harness Depot, a leather-works store down past the new newspaper, the *Trinidad Enterprise*. More houses were going up every day, seemed like. Hammering and sawing was damn near nonstop. Caleb York called it progress. Tulley never knew progress was so loud before.

As he walked along the boardwalk — with his shotgun cradled in his arms, which was fitting as he thought of the scattergun as his baby — Tulley found himself suddenly shivering. Then his teeth began to chatter.

He had realized the night was a mite nippy, but he didn't own a coat at this juncture — just hadn't got around to it, and anyway, New Mexico winters were brisk but never bitter, in his experience. Just like the summers around Trinidad never got so hot a man hardly ever noticed he was sweating.

The general darkness of the night — the blackness of the sky somehow giving off white flakes — was broken only by the glow of the Victory Saloon's windows. Tulley knew his boss was in that cheery den of iniquity right now, playing cards with the town fathers. The deputy picked up the pace, heading over there.

It was cold enough tonight that the inner doors of the saloon were shut over the batwing ones that normally welcomed in the weather as well as customers. Tulley got himself through this barrier and into the town's lone water hole, though before long, as Trinidad's population increased from three-hundred-some to who-knew-how-many, that would likely change.

As for the Victory, what with so many ranches around, and thirsty wayfarers passing through, few small-town slopshops had more to offer. The ceilings were high embossed tin with kerosene chandeliers, the walls fancy gold-and-black brocade decorated by saddles and spurs hung up like trophies. The oak bar went on forever, with white-shirt, black-bowtie bartenders ready to slake your thirst from a row of bourbon and rye bottles imported all the way from Denver.

As for Tulley, he was reformed of such temptation. He came in only for sarsaparilla or to see Sheriff York, who spent many an off-hour here — mostly for poker and faro, though some said he spent time upstairs with Miss Rita, too. This Tulley did not consider his business.

Not that he'd have blamed the sheriff. Rita Filley was one fine-looking, dark-eyed specimen of the female species, hair as black as a raven's wing, piled up on top of her pretty head, her full bosom about half on display in that green-and-black silk gown, waist tiny but hips flaring out. Birthing a child would have come natural to that one, iffen she wasn't already looking after the dusty cowboys at the bar, each with one foot on the rail and a spittoon nearby to feed.

Miss Rita — who'd inherited the place from her late sister, Lola, another fine-looking female, but who'd got herself killed by a snake whose rattle Caleb York silenced

21

once and for all — was standing with her arms folded on that natural shelf she carried around with her, looking on with a smile you couldn't read as she stood peeking at the sheriff's poker hand.

Business was slow, no surprise midweek like this. The roulette, chuck-a-luck, and wheel-of-fortune stations were all quiet, the piano silent on its little stage by the teeny dance floor, vacant right now. A few dance hall gals, in their fancy silk and feathers, sat bored. These were not soiled doves, at least not no more. Miss Rita had ended that practice not long after she took over for her dead sister.

House dealer Yancy Cole, a mustached, fancy-hat riverboat gambler working on dry land now, had a poker game going, too — cowhands and clerks. Next table over, near the stairs up to Miss Rita's quarters, was where Caleb York sat playing poker with six members of the Citizens Committee: portly, bespectacled Dr. Albert Miller; skinny, pop-eyed druggist Clem Davis; bulky, blond, mustached mercantile man Newt Harris; slight and slicked-up Mayor Jasper Hardy (Tulley's barber); bald but mutton-chopped Clarence Mathers, hardware store owner; and the new bank president, smallish, white-haired Peter Godfrey, who'd been installed in the position by Raymond L. Parker of Denver, who had holdings in Trinidad.

Caleb York himself, known throughout the Southwest as both a former Wells Fargo detective and a deadly gunhand, was big and lean and rawboned, clean-shaved with light blue eyes that had a lazy look that belied the man. His hair was brown with some red in it, and his jaw jutted some, as if daring some fool to take a poke at it.

When Tulley had first seen Caleb York ride in, with no idea who this was, the man seemed a dude with his citified duds, not so much the new-looking black coat and trousers, but them hand-tooled boots and the shirt with pockets on the front. And pearl buttons all the way down!

York was wearing that very shirt right now, and also the same curled-brim, cavalry-pinch, black hat, pushed back on his head as if not to put pressure on his brain whilst he was concentrating on his cards. In such wintery weather as this, the sheriff — though a county man, he handled the marshal tasks in town at the Citizens Committee's direction — left his shorter frock coat behind and went out in a rifle-length frock woolen coat. That coat was hanging on a wall peg just inside the Victory's door.

As Tulley approached the table where York

and them city muckety-mucks was playing, Miss Rita noticed the deputy and met him a few feet away.

"I'm going to guess," the lovely saloon owner said with a smile like she was being lightly tickled, "that you would prefer coffee to sarsaparilla tonight, Mr. Tulley."

He liked the way she put "mister" in front of his name. He dusted snow from his shoulder, like dandruff got out of hand, and said, "I surely would like some of that there java you be known for, far and wide."

The smile settled in one pretty cheek, dimpling it. "Well, I don't think my fame for making coffee has reached much beyond our city limits. But I will be glad to summon you a cup."

"Thank ye kindly, ma'am."

The sheriff had heard Tulley's voice and, as druggist Davis shuffled the cards in preparation for dealing them, Caleb York said, "Cold night out there, Deputy?"

Tulley shuffled over, his misshapen excuse for a hat in his hands. "Mite nippy, yessir."

"Coffee's a good idea." York gathered his cards, looked at them. Tulley hovered. The sheriff added, "Is there something else, Deputy?"

"I wonder iffen I might ask a favor of ye."

"If you make it quick you might."

24

"It be colder than a witch's teats out there, as you likely gathered, walkin' over. I wondered . . . could I borrow that frock coat of yorn?"

"Why, are you shivering out there?"

"Indeed I am. Teeth chatterin' like that girl Carmen's god-darn castanets over at the cantina."

"Your teeth don't seem to be chattering now."

"No, sir. Miss Rita keeps it nice and cozy-warm in here. But inside the Victory ain't where I make my nightly rounds."

"Open for a dollar," Caleb York said, and tossed some chips in, then turned to Tulley. "Go ahead and take the coat. I guess I can make it back to the office in my shirtsleeves without freezing, when I'm done here."

"Thank ye kindly, Sheriff!"

Miss Rita called to Tulley and he met her over at the bar, where he drank the coffee between two boys from the Bar-O, who were not having coffee. When he put the cup down and started to dig in a pocket for a coin, burly bartender Hub Wainwright waved that off as unnecessary. Tulley never paid for sarsaparilla either, but he always tried. Seemed impolite not to.

He was helping himself to the frock coat from its wall peg when the sheriff — someone was dealing again — called out, "Tulley! Come back over here."

Tulley in the coat — oversize on him, particularly the broad shoulders, getting him some smiles from bystanders that he chose to ignore — went over to see what Caleb York wanted. The garment almost touched the ground (whereas on York it would only barely meet midcalf).

The sheriff took off his black, cavalry-pinched hat and handed it to his deputy. "Here," he said. "Wear this. That thing you call a hat will blow away in that wind."

"Thank ye, Sheriff!" Tulley put the black hat on with one hand and stuffed the wadded-up headgear he'd been wearing into a pocket of the frock coat.

This evoked more amusement on the faces of the other patrons of the Victory, but no outright laughter. Say what you will about Tulley, he was now a man all in black with a shotgun in his arms.

Tulley exited the Victory and continued on his rounds. Before long he was checking on the street of facing houses that had grown up behind the businesses on this side of Main Street. Nothing had gone in on the other side of Main yet. That would come, with the railroad.

The houses back here were all quiet and

26

no lamps glowed in windows. In the sheriff's long black frock coat, Tulley blended right in with the snow-flecked dark. He still had the other side of Main Street to check, but first he would traverse the alley behind the businesses. On the other side of the alley were houses as well as businesses of a sort that didn't require a storefront. This included a rooming house like the one where Miss Rita had her saloon gals stay, ever since the Victory closed its second-floor bordello. There were also privies back there, one of which he used to divest himself of that cup of coffee, careful the sheriff's coat did not drag and get itself unclean.

When he emerged from that privy in the alley, he found himself right behind the Victory. On his way around to the front of the saloon, to go in and report to the sheriff and wangle himself another cup of coffee, Tulley tucked down his hat and lowered his head as he walked into a wind that was tossing snow in his face like a bride and groom getting pelted with rice outside a church.

His head was down that way when somebody fired at him, twice, blasts that shattered the night silence, and Jonathan Tulley — scattergun tumbling from a grip gone limp — fell on his face to the boardwalk just outside the Victory, the long black frock

27

coat covering him like a protective blanket, even as snowflakes dusted it and red pooled.

Shortly after his deputy, Jonathan Tulley, exited the Victory in the frock coat the sheriff had loaned him, Caleb York started having a run of bad luck.

Normally, with these town fathers, he would either win substantially or hold his own. So far tonight the latter had been the case. Then bad cards came flying at him unbidden and, hand after hand, good cards chose someone else to bless. No special someone — everybody but York was taking winnings in, time to time, no cheating — but that was when the evening had started going wrong.

The only thing different tonight at the table was the addition of banker Godfrey, in his first time playing with the little group. Admittedly this portly, distinguished-looking newcomer — brought to town by Raymond Parker to run the First Bank of Trinidad — was showing himself to be a smart, shrewd card player. But certainly no smarter nor better than Caleb York.

Yet if York had learned anything in his going on forty years above ground, it was that a man's luck could change on the turn of a card. He'd had his share of luck, both good and bad, though truth be told sometimes those two things could mingle.

His skill and speed with a sidearm had aided him as a Wells Fargo detective who had been sent to track bad men down and bring them back in that traditional dead or alive fashion. And when York consistently came back alive with his quarry slung over a saddle dead, that was skill and speed, yes, but luck was also involved in life-and-death confrontations, always.

So that was good luck, right?

Only earning a reputation as a fast gun wasn't really lucky at all. York had too often been backed into corners by challengers who required him shooting . . . killing . . . his way out. So a while back, when a false story blew across the Southwest saying that Caleb York had been gunned down, he had embraced the lie. When he'd first ridden into Trinidad, on his way to a Pinkerton job waiting in San Diego, California, he was blissfully free of the burden of his own identity.

Just another stranger passing through.

But then he'd gotten himself tangled up with a corrupt local sheriff and an honest ranch owner with a beautiful daughter, and now somehow — not even a year later — he was wearing the badge of the vile sheriff he'd been forced to kill. After that, his reputation as the "legendary" Caleb York had made him a local hero and some kind of fool tourist attraction ("Yes, Willie boy — that's *him*! That's Caleb York himself from the dime novels!").

And no question York was making good money as county sheriff — without a marshal in town, he was handling that role as well, getting a share of the taxes he collected plus rewards for bagging wanted men, not to mention all kinds of perquisites piled on to keep him happy.

And in Trinidad.

Right now the white-haired banker was dealing a hand and, suddenly, York's luck seemed to change. First one ace, then another, then a king . . . then *another* king! Two high-riding pairs! He drew a single card.

Another ace.

Aces full.

Two others at the table seemed to have drawn decent hands as well, and when the time came for the players to show their cards, the pot was piled with chips — probably twenty dollars; no fortune maybe, but real money.

The banker had a flush in hearts. The druggist had his own full house — queens over deuces. Those two hands had driven that pot to its lovely, plump, current state. And now Caleb York, with his aces and kings, was pulling in all those chips.

"Looks like my luck has finally turned," he told his fellow players, grinning but trying not to seem too damn smug about it.

That was when came the two gunshots, right outside, so close they almost seemed to be in the saloon with them. Barroom chatter ceased and a church-like quiet settled in an instant.

Then York was on his feet with his Colt Single Action Army .44 in hand, the silence filled by the sound of his boots slapping the wooden floor as he headed to the doors. The batwings opened onto a shallow entryway, with double doors that had been shut to keep out the cold but not customers, easy enough to push through.

There, as if he'd been tossed from a horse and dropped on the Victory's doorstep, was the sprawl of Jonathan Tulley, the long black coat draped on his skinny form like a shroud.

York crouched at his fallen deputy's side. The loaned hat had been knocked off the man and York rather absentmindedly retrieved it and put it back on. He retrieved the shotgun Tulley had dropped, as well.

Behind the two lawmen the other card players gathered, as well as bartender Wainwright and a few rubbernecking cowboys. Doc Miller pushed through and knelt beside York, who got out of the way but stayed down there, literally on his toes.

Then Rita Filley was hovering, asking, "Is he . . . ?"

"Breathing," the doctor said, his voice midrange and husky. "For now. Hub!"

The bartender pushed through. "Yes, sir?"

"You help the sheriff here carry Deputy Tulley over to my surgery."

"Yes, sir!"

The bartender took Tulley's ankles, and York — after passing the shotgun off to Rita for safekeeping — hooked his hands up under the deputy's shoulders. The shooting victim was as unconscious as a stone, the activity not getting a whimper out of him. Leaving a blood-droplet trail, the two men, led by the doctor, made the walk quickly and even whisked what seemed to be a corpse up the outer steps outside the formidable bank building and in through the doc's office with its waiting area and, beyond that, into the small surgery. York and Wainwright, at the doc's direction, deposited Tulley on the mahogany examination table.

The bartender was thanked and excused while York helped the doctor get the long frock coat off the deputy and together they got him out of his clothing. This exposed two wounds under the left rib cage. Both bubbled blood.

The doc put a hand on York's shoulder. "I'll take it from here. Go back to the game."

"Hell with the game!"

"Then take it to your room at the hotel. I'll send for you."

York's head shake was firm. "No. I'll be in your office if you need me or have anything to report."

Sighing, nodding, Miller was climbing out of his suit coat. "Do as you like."

"Are we going to lose him?"

"I need a closer look. No talk now, Caleb. Sit out there and wait. Pray if you like."

"Not much for that, Doc."

Miller was hanging his suit coat on a coat tree. "Not a bad time to start."

York went out into the waiting room, taking with him the long frock coat he'd loaned Tulley. He held it in his arms as if it needed comforting. The chair he took was the doctor's own, behind the desk; the seat was padded and the thing rocked, which gave the sheriff something to do. He sent a prayer up. It was an awkward, inarticulate thing, and if God was listening, York hoped the Entity was in a New Testament mood. There would be time enough for York's own Old Testament one.

By the time the sheriff checked his pocket watch, over an hour had crawled by. York's heartbeat had slowed to normal now, and he'd taken time to examine the coat. It had four holes in it, which told him something.

Finally the doc came out, his hair mussed as if he'd been trying to tear it out, his shirtsleeves rolled up with the smell of alcohol on his flesh and blossoms of red here and there on the white shirt like a careless print.

"He's not awake," the doctor said, standing by his desk and looking down at the man sitting in his chair. "But Tulley's breathing regular. Lost some blood, but I have him cleaned up and stitched, fore and aft. Bullets went in and out, which is a small blessing, anyway."

"I know they did."

This seemed to mildly amuse the medical man. "How did you come to make that diagnosis, Caleb?"

With one hand, York hefted the heavy cloth coat. "Four bullet holes and two gunshots. You think anything vital got hit?"

Miller shook his head. "Appears not.

Seems to have missed his lung. Don't believe we'll risk a transfusion. I've seen chills and pains and even death set in, when that doesn't go right."

York nodded. "What's next?"

"I'm not going to move him just yet. When I do, I'll get help. I have that room with an extra bed in my apartment here, where I can keep an eye on him. With any luck, he'll be conscious by morning and I'll send for you. Maybe he saw who did this."

"Good." York got to his feet.

"Tulley's a harmless soul," the doc said, sighing, making room for York to pass. "Never hurt a fly that I know of."

"Not true," York said. "He killed one of the Rhomers, when they came after me not so long ago."

The doc frowned in thought. "Aren't all the Rhomer boys dead?"

"I certainly hope so. But this isn't about Tulley."

"What, was he shot for sport?"

York shook his head. "It's a dark, snowy night, Doc. And he was in my hat and long coat."

The doctor's eyes flared. "I'm a fool! Should've figured that from the outset."

"You had your hands full. Mind was elsewhere."

35

York put on his hat and tipped it to the doctor. Then he gathered up the frock coat.

Some of Tulley's blood was on it, soaking it in places. Already it was getting dry and crinkly and black. The Chinese laundry would get rid of the stain, but Caleb York would not have the local seamstress patch the holes. They were a reminder.

A reminder of who the intended victim almost certainly was.

York put on the coat and went out into the cold.

CHAPTER TWO

The night before the shooting of Deputy Jonathan P. Tulley on its doorstep, the Victory had unknowingly hosted a little group whose conversation over cards would spawn that crime and others.

Rita Filley, the saloon's beauteous owner, had only one house dealer on staff, Yancy Cole, with a second table available to patrons who were restricted to nickel and dime play. The city fathers who frequently took over that spare table were not held to that general rule, and pots could get healthy indeed. But if a group of cowhands and clerks was playing, any coin higher than a twenty-cent piece would earn the wrath of bartending bouncer Hub Wainwright.

On this very slow weekday night, Yancy's table had a quartet of cowboys from various local ranches playing. This time of year was slow even on weekends, most spreads laying off as many as half their hands till spring.

The other table with its four players was enough of an oddity that Rita herself would wander over from time to time, casting a wary eye. Low speaking would then get louder and strictly be poker talk — raises or bets or folds or what-have-you.

What was unusual were the three non-locals — bigger men than most cowboys (a smaller size rider was easier on a rancher's horses). Their attire was an odd commingling of city and country. Cowhands tended to wear homemade cotton shirts and woolen trousers, the latter often with stitched buckskin across the butt and inner thighs to prevent wearing out from rubbing against a saddle all day.

These three wore black suits, but without the necktie a merchant or clerk might wear, and overall more threadbare than most; meanwhile, their weathered hats were tall-crowned and wide-brimmed like a buckaroo's, which might well brand them as drifters.

The fourth at the table was a local merchant, though a relative newcomer to Trinidad — his business, Maxwell Boots, Saddle, and Harness Depot, had only been open since November. He was well-dressed, in a similar but unfrayed black suit, and wore a light blue cravat. Bliss Maxwell was thirty-eight and prematurely gray, his face pleasant but stopping short of handsome, his wide-set, light blue eyes his only striking feature and going well with the neckwear.

The three strangers in the black, well-worn suits were Frank Fender, Jake Warlow, and Ned Sivley.

Frank "Moody" Fender was a broad-shouldered sort, if somewhat stooped, hunching in on himself as if the dark attitude that earned him his nickname was forcing that upon him. His small dark eyes lurked under a shelf of forehead, over a knob of a nose, a beard surrounding thick lips. He smoked a crooked cheroot, and looked a bit stupid. Which he was. Also he was at least as crooked as the cheroot.

Next to him — of the four at the table playing careless cards, often not even betting — Jake Warlow smiled as if he were holding four of a kind. Warlow was wolfishly handsome, and the best groomed of the trio, his suit and shirt a trifle cleaner than Fender's and Sivley's. He also looked smarter than his saddle-tramp companions, and was.

In the next chair, Ned Sivley sat skinny as a scarecrow and twice as frightful, a cadaverous-looking lunger with a nasty cough. Sivley was a gray man — of hair, of eye, of complexion, of scraggly beard — and his ambition in life was to die in bed in a warm clime with enough money to never work again. So far he was getting the dying part right, but accumulating money had eluded him.

None of these drifters had known Bliss Maxwell before. If anyone had seen the little group gathering, to play some nickel-dime poker, they would have thought the local merchant had sat down with the trio by accident. No one but these four themselves knew that Sivley had earlier approached Bliss in the saddle shop and given him a message from a mutual acquaintance. That message had included meeting here at the Victory at eight o'clock p.m. It was eight-thirty now.

The leader of the three strangers in black was not present. He was Lucas "Burn 'Em" Burnham, a notorious outlaw whose appellation came from his rampaging days with the infamous bushwackers known as Quantrill's Raiders. And Burnham was the common link between the drifters and the merchant.

Unknown to any others in Trinidad, Bliss Maxwell had once been one of Burnham's gang, not in raiding days but after the war, when stagecoaches were the prey. While

Burnham had been caught and jailed, Maxwell had managed to steer clear of the law and never served a day.

For the past ten years, in fact, Bliss Maxwell — whose real name was not that — had been a more or less honest business-man and upstanding citizen in the South-west, having invested his ill-gotten gains to start over. This was not an unusual practice in the post–Civil War West.

Maxwell had run a general store in Santa Fe that did well for a time, but when competition came in, as the town got big enough to support retailers with specialties like clothing or groceries or hardware, his business had suffered. He sold out to a competitor and hired a top Mexican saddle maker to go along with the harness-making skills he himself had picked up, and moved to Trinidad.

The four men chatted, speaking low. Enough space was between the two tables of card players that being overheard was not a problem, unless you got careless. These men didn't. For the most part, only Jake Warlow — who had a deep, mellow, almost soothing voice at odds with his feral counte-nance — did most of the talking. In the absence of Burnham, Jake spoke for him.

"You would get a full share," Warlow said,

41

shuffling the cards.

"I don't know," Maxwell said.

Sivley coughed into a handkerchief dotted with red and black — fresh and dried blood. "You should count yourself lucky, store-keep."

Maxwell's cool blue eyes found Sivley's gray, gray-eyed face. "Lucky how? What would *you* be risking?"

"Just my life," Sivley said, stuffing the bloody handkerchief away, as if to hide the fact that his years remaining weren't worth all that much at this stage.

But Fender put in, "All of us risk life and limb, and all you got to do? Is hardly nothing. Truth be told, I was against it."

Maxwell frowned, absentmindedly pulling in cards Warlow had just dealt him. "Against what?"

Fender's sneer was nasty. "Givin' you a full *share,* you damn fool."

"If I have to put up with *you* for very long," Maxwell said, the former outlaw in the merchant coming out, "I should get *more* than a share."

"Gentlemen," Warlow said, and smiled his handsome smile. "Who wants cards?"

They went through the pretense of play-ing draw, and between bets, Maxwell said,

42

"Why isn't Burnham here making his own case?"

Sivley made a face and said, "Can't you figure that out yourself?"

"No." Maxwell shrugged. "He's distinctive looking, I grant you. But he's not famous. He's not President Grant."

"Grant is dead," Fender said.

Maxwell frowned. "Grover Cleveland isn't, but nobody would recognize *him,* either, much less Burn 'Em."

Warlow said, "Somebody in this town would."

A tall man, lean yet broad of shoulder, came in wearing a long black frock coat, which he hung up on a peg inside the door. He was still in black underneath as well, including his hat.

"That's him," Maxwell said.

The other three card players had a good look. Nothing suspicious about that — unlike President Cleveland, Caleb York was somebody people might well recognize. Good likenesses of him had appeared on the front of dime novels, and anyway it was well known that York was sheriff of Trinidad County.

"He's a tall one," Warlow admitted, looking at his latest hand of cards.

"Wears that .44 low," Sivley said, "like a

43

damn gunfighter."

"That's what he *is*, fool," Fender said.

"Keep callin' me fool, Moody," Sivley said with a nasty smile. "See where it gets you."

"Go to hell." Fender was looking at his cards, too.

Sometimes men who rode together or worked a ranch side by side would tell another to go to hell in a good-natured way. Fender's remark read different. These were men who put up with each other's company.

"Okay," Maxwell said, even softer than before, almost a whisper. "You wanted York pointed out. I pointed him out. Now what?"

"Play cards," Warlow advised.

They did this for a while. They noticed that Sheriff York sat at one of the small tables between them and the door, having a drink with the bosomy looker in dark blue silk who ran the place. They did not hear the conversation between the bar owner and the sheriff.

What they specifically didn't hear was Rita Filley asking Caleb York, "Do you know those three characters playing nickel-dime poker with Bliss Maxwell?"

Without looking at them, York said, "No. But I don't care for the cut of their jib. They don't punch cows for a living and they sure as hell aren't drummers."

44

York meant salesmen, not musicians.

"They're drifters," she said, "if you ask me."

Of course, he hadn't, but York did ask her, "What's your beef with them?"

"Nothing. But they don't look like the type to play that kind of poker."

"What kind of poker is that? Playing for loose change, you mean?"

She shook her head. "They aren't really playing. They're paying no attention to their cards. Just talking. What about, is what I want to know." She leaned forward and York managed to keep his eyes off her neckline. "We've never been robbed here, Caleb, but I'm wondering if tonight's the night."

"I'll settle in next to them," he said, starting to rise.

She stopped him with a hand on a wrist. "What I really want to know is . . . what's *Maxwell* doing with them?"

York sat himself back down. "Did they come in together?"

"No," she said. "The saddle shop man was having a beer at the bar. Those three sauntered in, looking around the place in a way thirsty customers don't usually look. Then one of them, the death-warmed-over character, nodded toward the bar and they approached Bliss. They spoke some, then he

45

guided them over to the empty table. Started playing for nothing much."

York thought that over. "I've been suspicious about more."

"You've also been suspicious about less. As long as they're here, Caleb? *You* be here, too, all right?" She squeezed his hand. "Then you can come upstairs, if you like. It has been a while."

"It has," he admitted.

Then he went over and settled into a free seat at Yancy's table. He kept an eye on the other table without really seeming to.

With York nearby, Bliss Maxwell and the three outlaws played without talk of anything but cards. Warlow won some money. Nobody else did. Half an hour or so passed.

Maxwell said, "I'd like to see our mutual friend."

Warlow nodded, said, "Good idea. He's waiting."

They were not aware that Caleb York had heard that and stored it away.

Then the card players got up and went out into the chilly night.

Over the archway entrance, its door shut tight against the cold, the words CANTINA DE TORO ROJO curved in red letters so faded they were almost orange. The two-story

46

adobe structure — its glass-free windows shuttered and bleeding yellow light around their edges — might have been an old church, the outpost of some long-forgotten mission. And one could certainly commune over wine here.

A bar with food did business below while an exposed wooden staircase along the right side of the building led to a tawdry heaven of small rooms where fallen amber angels blessed customers for modest offerings. Few of the worshipers lived in the small, shabby barrio whose central lane led to the cantina. The believers making this impure pilgrimage, after dark anyway, were mostly cowboys — white and black and brown — as well as proper town men, who felt confident that any other proper town men they encountered would keep all impropriety to themselves.

Muffled talk and the strumming of a guitar could barely be heard by the four men who had walked up Main Street from the Victory to the livery stable end of town, with the sheriff's jailhouse office at right and the Mexican section at left. At the leather-glazed hitch rail out front stood four horses, shuffling in place whenever the wind would pick up. A pleasantly pudgy señorita of about fifteen was leading a vaquero client twice her age up those stairs.

Within the cantina waited the leader of the three drifters, a man who had once led another thieving band that included an unreformed Bliss Maxwell. Luke Burnham — a bottle of tequila before him as well as glasses for himself and the coming guests — wore an old military jacket, a practice not unusual even twenty years after the war. But his was a heavy gray Confederate coat, not often seen now, though still a damn good choice for winter weather.

Since the war, Burnham had been two things: an outlaw and a convict. His distinctive scarred face had got him identified when he'd started robbing stages, and as a notorious raider who had ridden with Quantrill. He had been tracked down by a Wells Fargo detective and served ten years for armed robbery at the Kansas State Pen. The only luck he'd had was getting nabbed for a holdup where no one had gotten killed, an exception in Burnham's practice, not the rule.

Warlow entered the cantina first, followed by Fender and Sivley, with Maxwell bringing up the rear, looking around him to see if any other townspeople were there who might recognize him. This was Maxwell's first visit to the cantina (he was seeing a young woman he'd met at a First Missionary Baptist social).

Their flat boots crunched on the straw-strewn floor. Only half a dozen patrons were present, including two Mexican cowboys and a black one playing three-handed poker, a genuine nickel-dime game. The restaurant aspect of the Red Bull (as most gringos called it) was closed though the odor of refried beans hung stubbornly in the air. A little guy in a big sombrero perched in a corner noodling flamenco-style guitar on a battered instrument.

The fat, balding bartender with a droopy bandido mustache gave the new customers an equally droopy-eyed nod as he wiped down the bar with a filthy rag. The yellow-painted walls were faded and so was a bullfighter mural near the guitarist.

A slender señorita in her ancient late twenties was fading, too; she sported a nest of dark hair and a surprisingly full bosom that was too much for her peasant blouse. Her ballooning black skirt swirled with red, green, and yellow petticoats as she danced to the music of a guitarist who seemed more interested in her than did the clientele. Mismatched tables and chairs seemed flung around haphazardly, though a few areas were lattice-worked off, and at a table in

49

one of those was where Burnham waited.

The table, meant for four, had chairs for five, one of which contained Burnham, who got slowly to his feet, his smile slow as well, as he held out a hand for Maxwell to shake. The former outlaw did so, finding a nervous smile to accompany a nod to his old gang leader.

"Sit, old friend," Burnham said, gesturing to the chair at his right.

The other men exchanged glances — normally their boss wasn't this polite or friendly. Generally the man was a cross between a military task master and a foul-tempered parent. But his followers considered him tough and fearless and daring as hell, so they put up with him.

Everybody sat, the leader last.

"Burn 'Em" Burnham's hair was dark and streaked gray, as was the beard he kept trimmed. He was as broad-shouldered as his man Moody, only with no stoop and, unlike that underling, was no stupe. He was considerably smarter even than ladies' man Warlow, and might have been one himself, such were his handsome features in their rough-hewn masculine manner. But a damned sword blade in battle had put a scar through an eye and left him mildly disfigured and half blind, the eye still there but

50

milky now.

Burnham served tequila all around. The glasses were squat things, not designed for shots, and the outlaw leader poured generously. Then he raised his glass in a thick-fingered hand and everyone followed suit. They drank.

"Nice and smooth and smoky," Burnham said with a smile. He put a hand on Maxwell's sleeve and his non-milky eye on the man's face. "I understand business has been slow."

Maxwell frowned, more in surprise than anything else. "Who told you that?"

"Friend Sivley," Burnham said, nodding toward the lunger. An unsettling smile flashed in the midst of the black-and-gray beard. "Ned here spoke to that *pelado* saddle maker of yours — Salazar? Some fine ones on display, Ned says, but not a sale in a month."

"It's a waiting game," Maxwell said, quietly defensive.

The smile flashed again. "You're waitin' for that railroad spur, and all the people it'll bring. You're waitin' for this bump in the road to blossom."

Maxwell shrugged, then nodded. "Juan Salazar is a first-rate saddle man. And I know everything there is to know about harness making. Between the two of us, we'll make a fortune someday."

Burnham lifted a forefinger. "Someday. Not this day. Or the next. How long can you hang on, old friend? How long will this bean-eater of yours stick, makin' fancy saddles with no asses to sit them?"

Maxwell shrugged again. "I have a decent stake. We can hold on."

Burnham sipped tequila. "You can really taste the agave," he said appreciatively. "Surprising good, for a craphole deadfall like this. You know, ol' compadre, you deserve better."

"Better than what?"

"Better than holdin' on for dear life. Better than chippin' away at your stake waiting for the gold rush to come. It would give me genuine pleasure to help you out of this fix."

"Help me out."

Burnham gestured with two open hands. "Surely would. We're gonna plump that stake of yours up, boy. You may *think* you're sittin' at a table in a low-down Mexie thirst parlor, but that's really *opportunity* knockin'."

Maxwell sipped his tequila. He flinched a little, indicating he didn't find it as smooth and sweet a drink as his old boss did. He said, "I did you a favor, Luke. I pointed out

Caleb York to your friends here. That's on the house. No charge whatsoever."

"Big of you."

"But couldn't you have pointed York out just as easy as I did?"

Burnham shook his head. "Not without riskin' him spotting me and wondering what I was doing in his town."

Maxwell looked at Burnham long and hard. "York's the one put you away, isn't he?"

"He is. You were already off on your own when the bastard picked up our trail. So he doesn't know you from Adam. You're just another honest storekeep to" — he spoke the next three words with sublime contempt — "Sheriff Caleb York."

Maxwell leaned closer to the man he'd once ridden for. "I don't know what exactly you're up to, Luke. Nor do I know what it is you want from me." He slammed a fist on the table and made the tequila glasses jump. "And I don't *want* to know."

Burnham, perhaps not liking Maxwell getting so tough — or the man's show of stubbornness — leaned back and folded his arms. In the Confederate coat he could have fallen out of a Mathew Brady tintype. "You might as well know, old friend. You might as well play. You're an accessory already, if they catch us."

"How so?"

A thick-fingered hand patted the air. "Don't get ahead of yourself, son. You hear me out. You don't like the sound, you don't like the monetary prospect, why, you just thank us for thinkin' of you and go along about your respectable way. And we will wish you the best, includin' the hope that you don't go bust before this here town goes boom."

Maxwell thought about that. Warlow smiled at Fender, who for all his surliness smiled back — both men knew their boss had the shopkeeper thinking. They were well aware that Burnham was a master at devil's bargains.

Finally Maxwell asked, "How much?"

"I have it on reliable authority that the Bank of Las Vegas, New Mexico Territory, keeps one hundred thousand dollars on hand. Paper money, mostly. Some hard coin, but with luck not too much to haul away."

Maxwell's eyes widened. It might have been the thought of all that money. Or of all that risk.

Or both.

Then Maxwell asked, "My share would be what?"

"Like my boys told you. Full share, son. That's in the neighborhood of twenty-thousand dollars, cash and coin. Tell me, Mr. Maxwell — do you think twenty thousand would tide you over till your ship comes in? Or I should say, train?"

Maxwell thought about it, but then shook his head. "I sell saddles. I don't sit them. My days doing . . . your kind of work are well behind me. I'm no road agent now. I rarely carry a gun, for pity's sake. Anyway, Las Vegas is too close to home."

Burnham laughed loud enough to attract attention. Then as eyes turned away from them, the outlaw leader uncrossed his arms and touched Maxwell's sleeve again.

"We're not enlisting volunteer troops, Mr. Maxwell. Your role is a most specific one. You're an unmarried man with living quarters above your business — the whole top floor, Mr. Sivley tells me. You know, this Mexican leather cutter of yours, he's a talkative sort. Maybe you should have a word with him."

Maxwell, starting to get it, nonetheless asked, "What's your point? What *is* my role?"

Burnham flipped a hand. For a man who hadn't worked an honest day in his life, that hand had a toilworn look. "The ride from

Las Vegas is no hardship. We can make it in a damn hurry, horses little the worse for wear."

"I'm listening."

His stare, with that milky eye, was a troubling thing. "I intend to come to Trinidad and spend a week or so with you as our host. You have a workshop out back, we understand, that can serve as a stable for our horses. The law will expect us to head for Mexico. We will wait for things to blow over, and then take our leave . . . leaving you to enjoy your share of the proceeds, with hardly any risk at all."

Maxwell goggled at him. "You would use my home, above my place of business, as your *hideout*?"

"Exactly right. And as I say, I doubt we'll need to stay any longer than a week. That's a handsome week's rent for a landlord, wouldn't you say?"

Maxwell was shaking his head, as if saying no, but his words indicated otherwise: "You'd need provisions . . . horses would require hay . . . I do have indoor plumbing, so you wouldn't be seen going to and from a privy. . . . But what would I tell Juan?"

"Why, does he bunk with you?"

"No! But he has a room in back on the first floor, till he can build a little house . . .

when . . ."

"When that train of yours comes in."
Burnham flipped another hand. "Well, give
him the week off. Send him on some er-
rand, buying leather or some such. It's not
like you're doing land-office business."

Maxwell was nodding now. "I could do
that. Of course . . . might look suspicious,
buying a week's food for all five of us."

Burnham smiled — the shopkeeper was
already thinking of the others at the table as
part of one group.

Warlow put in, "Buy dry provisions.
Things you might purchase in quantity
anyhow. Flour. Cornmeal. I make a mean
flapjack."

"Jerky and such," Fender suggested.

Sivley said to Burnham, speaking as if
Maxwell wasn't even there, "Do we really
need some damn fool merchant? Why not
just hie for Mexico?"

"It's what's expected."

Suddenly Fender had doubts, too. "If we
aim to do what they don't expect, what's
wrong with heading north? We know people
Colorado way."

"No," Burnham said. "Not unless Mr.
Maxwell here doesn't want twenty thousand
dollars."

Maxwell was just sitting there.

"You're already an accessory," Burnham reminded him.

The merchant frowned. "You said that before. Why, because you talked to me about all this? I'd just deny it."

"No. Because you pointed out Caleb York to my men here."

"So what?"

"So," Burnham said with a shrug, "we're going to kill him."

Maxwell's eyes widened and his mouth made an O. It made Burnham smile before sipping tequila again.

Now Maxwell was squinting at his old boss. He said, "Why do that?"

"Well, if we're holed up in this town, I don't want Caleb York out there poking around, wondering if we might be hiding out in his damn county somewheres." Then the man in the Confederate jacket shrugged, rather grandly. "Also, that's part of the attraction."

Maxwell, not following, asked, "What is?"

"Killing that son of a bitch."

Before long, all four outlaws and their newly recruited gang member were out in the chill, walking through the sleeping barrio. Burnham and his men had paid to spend the night in the nearby livery with their animals — it was known that Caleb

York had a room at the Trinidad House Hotel, so staying there was out.

Just as the five men were about to emerge from the barrio, Burnham — in the lead, of course — put a hand on Maxwell's shoulder.

"Who is that?" the outlaw leader asked.

Coming out of the sheriff's office across the way was a bony, bandy-legged figure wearing a dark flannel shirt, gray woolen pants, red suspenders and work boots, under-dressed for weather this frosty.

Maxwell noted the deputy starting out on his nightly rounds.

"That's nobody," he said.

CHAPTER THREE

The morning after the shooting of Deputy Jonathan P. Tulley, Sheriff Caleb York — wearing the long black frock coat with its bullet holes and bloodstains, the brim of his cavalry-pinched black hat tugged down — moved along the boardwalk like a wraith emerging from the whispering snow.

Trinidad wearing white made something strange and strangely lovely out of the little Main Street, the way York saw it. He'd wintered plenty of places in the Southwest and rarely had weather like this found any of them. Certainly he hadn't expected such a thing in New Mexico, at least not until he saw the wire from the Territorial governor that had gone out to sheriffs and marshals telling of a blizzard underway north of them that seemed headed their direction.

The warning included no suggestions of how those lawmen were to address the coming cold — this part of the country had not, in recent years anyway, had a storm like this to deal with. If Tulley were up and around, York would have dispatched his deputy to go door to door — businesses and homes alike — and advise stocking up on provisions and then staying indoors until this beast literally blew over. Perhaps further suggesting they gather any available firewood and get it inside, to keep warmth going in the potbellies of their stoves.

But Tulley wasn't available for such duty, and anyway a surprising number of citizens were out and about, bundled up and walking along the boardwalk on both sides of Main, taking in the wintery sight of snow coating the already sand-covered street (brought over from the nearby Purgatory River to keep dust down in more typical weather). They blinked and brushed white flakes away as they gaped and goggled at awnings and rooftops already lined with snow and windowsills and hitching posts similarly snow edged.

A few merchants, in jolly moods as if an old-fashioned Christmas had arrived a month or so late, were out front of their shops with brooms, sweeping snow away, like it would do any good. Right now Trinidad was enjoying this change of pace in its weather, the snowfall steady but not unpleasant, wind swirling the stuff but not driving it. An artist at a window working in watercolor or oil might be trying right now to capture the scenic beauty of it all. Meanwhile the citizens who the sheriff knifed through on the boardwalk seemed to be memorizing their town so that, in a more typical snow-free winter, they might remember it.

York stopped at the café for coffee, stamping his feet and waving snow off his hat before heading in. One might have expected the unpretentious little restaurant's half a dozen tables, with their red-and-white checkered cloths, to be filled, and certainly a cup of Arbuckles' in this cold would seem called for. But the citizenry were out and about enjoying the novel conditions.

The sheriff hung the long coat on a peg inside the door but left his hat on, pushed back some. No wind to fight in here.

The place had a homey feel, nothing like the Victory, whose free lunches were the café's major competition. The wallpaper was yellow-and-white floral and might have been in a sitting room, and in one corner were some comfortable chairs with a table piled with books for the reading and relaxing pleasure of customers. Right now no one was doing either.

Fred, the owner and main waiter, came over in his usual white apron, a slender, bald, elaborately mustached man who brought an entire pot of coffee for the sheriff as well as a white-enameled tin cup. The two men exchanged nods and slight smiles.

"Shame about Tulley," Fred said, shaking his head.

"Shame," York agreed.

He was not surprised word had got around town about the shooting, as there had been plenty of witnesses there at the Victory when Tulley fell just beyond its portals. What York needed now were more witnesses, and not those who'd been in the saloon but anyone who heard the shots and had gone quickly to a window. That would be his first order of business today — seeking such people out.

Such door-knocking and routine interviews, of residents of the living quarters over businesses (usually their owners, but sometimes employees), was the side of detective work that, going back to his Wells Fargo days, York had never relished. But such tedium came with the territory.

He was pouring his second cup of coffee when Rita Filley came in, wearing a two-piece hunter-green woolen dress with a black velvet collar. Plenty warm for your average New Mexico winter, she was under-dressed for this one. Snow dusted her, and she paused inside the door to brush it off as best she could, her dark eyes searching for, then finding York.

She rushed over, in a rustle of cloth, as he stood and pulled a chair out for her. Sitting, getting out of a pair of velvet gloves that matched the collar of her dress, she was flushed with cold but wore no face paint, her natural beauty always something of a surprise to York.

"How is Jonathan?" she asked, one of the few people in town — or presumably any-where else — who didn't call the deputy just "Tulley."

"I haven't stopped by the doc's just yet," York said, pouring coffee into a cup Fred had dropped off for Rita.

She drank eagerly, almost greedily; like the sheriff, she took it black.

York added, "If Tulley took a bad turn, I'd know about it."

Concern in the big brown eyes in the heart-shaped face turned to frustration-tinged anger. "Do you have any thoughts about who might have done this thing? And why *Jonathan*?"

He had to mull that a moment. Then he

decided there was no reason not to tell her. His pointing finger drew her eyes to the coat hanging inside the door — the two bullet holes and the patches of blackened blood in back were easily seen.

She showed no reaction. "So your coat on your deputy means *you* may have been the target."

"Strong possibility." He nodded at her cup. "You have coffee at the Victory. Did you stop for breakfast?"

"No. I was looking for you."

Finding him this time of the morning had taken no great deductive powers on her part — York either had breakfast at the hotel where he kept a room, or here at the café.

"Looking for news of my deputy," he said.

"No. Well, yes. But I have something on my mind that could pertain. It may be nothing, or . . ."

"It might be something. What is it?"

She sipped coffee, then leaned toward him. Though the place was underpopulated, the woman seemed to want to keep this private.

"Remember night before last," she said, "when those three out-of-towners sat down for poker with Bliss Maxwell — the latest addition to the Citizens Committee?"

That was the as yet unofficial town council, headed up by the mayor and including the most prominent merchants in town, as well as the new bank president.

"I remember," he said.

"More I think about it," Rita said, looking past him, "the more I get the feeling they *knew* him. I didn't see who approached who — I just looked over and the four of them, Maxwell and these three characters, were playing poker."

York frowned. "The more you think about it, you said. Why are you still thinking about this two days later?"

What she said wasn't exactly an answer to his question. "I have served a lot of men at the Victory these past months and I can tell when someone walks into my place wearing trouble."

"They didn't cause any trouble while I was there."

"No." The dark, pretty eyes narrowed. "But after you left, I stepped outside for some air. It was before the snow started and I was just enjoying the brisk feel of this weather, which hadn't got out of hand yet."

"And it is going to *really* get out of hand." He told her about the warning wire from the Territorial governor. Then he continued: "But you were saying . . . after you stepped outside?"

66

She nodded, sipped more coffee, said, "I saw the four of them again. The three out-of-towners and Bliss Maxwell."

"Doing what?"

"They were down the street, just outside the barrio, standing across from your office at the jail. Just gathered there talking. Nothing unusual, really. I merely figured they'd been over at the cantina for some more drinking and such."

He smiled a little. "The Red Bull is serving its customers entertainment in ways you no longer provide."

She smiled a little, too. "That's right. Our girls just dance and encourage drinking, these days. Thanks to our prudish new sheriff."

That wasn't entirely the case. He had since learned Rita'd been planning to divest herself of the upstairs brothel at the Victory even before he first brought the subject up.

"So," York said, "if Bliss and his three poker companions were just having a night out on the town, what made all of this linger in your memory?"

"They weren't alone," she said, her eyes tight now. "There was a fifth man. A man wearing an old Confederate military jacket."

York leaned in. "Could it just be a gray coat you mistook?"

67

"No." She shook her head slowly, silently. Then she said, "I . . . I walked down a ways. On the boardwalk, kind of tucked against the storefronts. Something about this seemed . . . *wrong*, somehow. It was a Rebel jacket, all right. And who wears a Reb jacket twenty years later?"

The back of his neck was tingling, but York said, "Well, such coats are good and warm in this inclement weather."

She was shaking her head again, but just slightly. Thoughtfully. "He was a tough-looking jasper, this fifth man. He wore a beard, trimmed close to his face. He was damn near as tall as you, Caleb."

"How close did you get?"

"Not right up on him."

"Could you recognize him?"

She thought about it. "If he was in that jacket, maybe. With his beard shaved off, not a chance. I didn't get that good a look. His features seemed regular. Not at all ugly. There may have been something funny about . . . his eyes."

"Funny? His eyes?"

"I had the impression they weren't the same color. Like one was dark, the other not. Again, I was not that close — I didn't hear a thing they said. And I believe I would have forgotten all about it, if . . ."

"If Deputy Tulley didn't have holes in him."

She nodded. "And if your coat didn't have holes in it, too."

He touched her hand. Squeezed. Smiled at her. She smiled at him.

She asked, "What now, Caleb?"

"I'm going to fetch a wanted poster from the office. I may know who it is you saw."

Now she clutched his hand. "Caleb, I'm sorry, but I didn't see this person well enough to recognize his image in a drawing or photograph."

"I understand. But even if you can't, I know someone who might."

Fifteen minutes later, York walked down the central lane of a quaintly snowy version of the barrio, which led to the two-story Cantina De Toro Rojo. During the day this citadel of sin was merely a rather grand version of the shabby abodes leading up to it, a snow-edged one now. No horses were tied up at the hitching rail and no one was going in or out.

Inside York found the place deserted but for its owner, Cesar, who was managing to look sweaty even in this cold weather, as he sat at a small table counting his money, making piles and stacks — coins and paper, dollars and pesos. Strips of black hair crossed his bald head, his eyes dark and half lidded, his mustache a limp droopy thing, his untucked shirt matching his trousers in their cream color and general bagginess.

York's boot scrunched across the straw-covered floor. He joined his unenthusiastic host at the table.

"*Mi casa es tu casa,* Sheriff York," Cesar said in a manner as practiced as it was insincere. "But we are not open for the business yet."

"I'm not here for beer or tequila or beans," the lawman said. He unrolled the wanted poster he'd plucked from the wall of his office and spread it out like a much-too-small tablecloth. "Has this man been a customer?"

The circular bore a rendering of the wanted man, but York — who not only had met the outlaw in question but had captured and sent him to prison — knew it to be accurate. The drawing was chest up, to give a sense of the Confederate officer's jacket this individual was known to wear, and the wanted man's roughly handsome, trimly bearded face, with its off-putting milky eye and saber scar through his eyebrow, made him unmistakable. The reward was one thousand dollars, a considerable bounty.

Lucas Burnham, also known as Luke Burnham and "Burn 'Em" Burnham, was wanted for robbery in various states of the union as well as several territories, including New Mexico, where he was also wanted for murder.

"Hay dinero?" Cesar asked, with a sudden, alert smile.

"If I find him," York said, nodding slowly, "and bring him in, dead or alive, likely the former, I will remember you, Cesar."

"Me recordarás bien?"

"I will remember you to the tune of one hundred dollars."

"I like this tune. I need do nothing but tell you if I have seen this man?"

"That's right. Has he been here?"

"Noche antes de la última," Cesar said, nodding quickly.

"Night before last," York said. "Since then?"

"No."

"Before then?"

"No."

"Who was he with?"

"Three men — not from here. Another man — *from* here, I think."

"Who?"

"No lo conozco."

"You're sure of that, Cesar?"

The cantina keeper nodded again. "Never at the Red Bull before. But he dress well. A

71

gringo."

"Was there any trouble with these men, night before last?"

"No."

"What did they do?"

"Talk. Drink. Much talk. Little drink."

York stood. "Okay. Thanks, Cesar. I may ask you to identify the local."

Cesar, still seated, raised his hands, palms out, as if giving himself up to the law. *"No quiero problemas!"*

"You won't have any. And I may not need you to identify him."

Cesar liked hearing that. "Do not forget my hundred dollars!"

"Why, would you let me?"

Cesar grinned, then went back to counting his money.

The saddle shop was next door to the office of the *Trinidad Enterprise* at the west end of Main, a wide, two-story, clapboard building of recent construction. York made his way there, down the boardwalk, the wind from the northwest held back some by the buildings. But the white stuff came down steady now, the flakes fat and wet and gathering.

The sheriff stomped the snow from his boots before going in the door under the white-lettered sign — MAXWELL BOOTS,

SADDLE, AND HARNESS DEPOT — and, not surprisingly, he found himself alone in the place with its proprietor. Immediately the musky scent of well-oiled leather tweaked York's nostrils, and he didn't mind a bit. It was one of those familiar, oddly comforting smells so evocative of the West. From the back, in the workshop, came the tapping of a mallet, likely Maxwell's Mexican saddle maker at work.

On counters left and right, within the rough-wood walls of the shop, were stacks of buckskin shirts and jackets, and an impressive array of varieties of rawhide, horsehair, and leather goods. Two beautifully hand-tooled saddles on furniture-quality stands were at left; another two strictly functional models were at right.

Bliss Maxwell stood in back of a glass display case that showed off ornate spade bits, vaquero spurs, and various silver goods. Maxwell wore professional black, including a string tie with a silver horse-head clasp, his gray hair more suited to an older man, his blandly inoffensive features set off by sky-blue eyes.

"You're my first customer today, Sheriff," Maxwell said. His voice was midrange; his tone struck York as friendlier than need be.

"Not a customer," York said. "I'm here on

73

my business, not yours."

"Nothing serious, I hope. I, uh, heard about your deputy. Is he going to be all right?"

"Time'll tell. It was an accident, you know."

Maxwell frowned, confused. "Accident? I heard he was shot!"

"He was shot wearing my coat." York took a step back and turned to show the rear of the garment and its bullet holes and caked blood. Then he turned and said casually, "The accident was somebody taking him for me."

Maxwell might have come around to meet York halfway, but the shop owner stayed behind the display case, which made the lawman walk to him. It seemed to York that the merchant, despite his cheerful tone, liked having something between him and the law.

"Those men you sat down to play poker with," York said, leaning an elbow casually on the display case, "night before last? They friends of yours?"

"No," Maxwell said, shrugging, apparently bewildered that he was being asked such a thing.

York cocked his head. "How did you happen to get into a game with them? They looked like fairly rough boys. Wore their irons gunfighter-style."

The shop owner shrugged again. "They struck up a conversation when I was ordering a beer. Somebody told them I ran this shop, and they had some interest in my saddles."

"So you socialized some, to smooth the way."

Maxwell smiled again. "That's right."

"Did you end up doing business with them?"

With a laugh, Maxwell said, "No. That's the last I saw of 'em. I even lost a dollar and a half to the stoop-shouldered gent."

"You get their names?"

Maxwell thought about that. "I, uh, think the stoop-shoulder was called Frank, and the slender fellow Ned Something. The other was Jake, I believe."

"You didn't get their surnames?"

Maxwell shook his head. "If any came up, I don't recall. It was just Frank, Ned, and Jake. As in, Frank's deal, Ned's pot, Jake folds."

York withdrew the rolled-up wanted circular from the deep right pocket of his frock coat. He smoothed it out on the display-case counter. "Have you seen this man in town?"

The shop owner studied the poster. No need to ask if he knew this outlaw's name, because it was in big, bold letters, alongside various aliases. Maxwell's eyes moved with thought.

Bliss Maxwell was wondering whether he'd been seen with Burnham, or so the sheriff figured.

"Yes," Maxwell said finally, nodding, eyes still on the circular, "he was friendly with those other three. He wasn't ever at the Victory that I know of. After the game broke up, the other three asked me along for a nightcap at the cantina. I sat with them and this wanted man, and we drank tequila and talked."

"About?"

He shrugged yet again. "About nothing. About everything. They wanted to know if the girl dancing at the cantina was available. I told them I'd heard the girls at de Toro Rojo were, yes, very available, at cheap enough a price. Or so I understood." His expression got serious and he looked down his nose at the sheriff. "I myself have never indulged."

"Did this one" — York tapped the face of the drawing of "Burn 'Em" Burnham — "ask about me?"

"No! Why should he?"

York offered a genial smile. "Because I sent him to Kansas State Penitentiary for ten years for armed robbery, and he served every day. And because he was in town the night before last, and then *last* night, as you'll recall, my deputy — wearing this coat of mine? Was shot down in the street."

Maxwell's complexion had turned damn near as white as his hair. "Sheriff, this wanted man was just someone I shared a drink with at the cantina! I never saw him before or since. They said they were leaving the next morning. If they were telling the truth, that bunch wasn't even in town when Deputy Tulley was shot! *Certainly* I haven't seen them."

"Well," York said easily, wanting to settle the shop owner back down, "if you do happen to run into them, I'd be obliged if you say nothing of our conversation this morning. I would steer a wide berth of them, were I you."

Maxwell raised a palm, as if taking the oath in court. "Yes, Sheriff York. That's good advice indeed. But should I see them, I will let you know. Straightaway."

York nodded. He glanced at the well-made objects in the display case. He looked around at the saddles and other merchandise.

"You should do well here, Mr. Maxwell," he said, nodding appreciatively. "*Very* well, when the Santa Fe spur comes in." He smiled. "Love the smell of the place. Leather has such an unmistakable scent. Strong. Like the odor that rolls off an outlaw . . . only pleasant."

York tipped his hat to the merchant, who smiled again, but this smile was a kind of curdled thing.

On the short walk to Doc Miller's office, York found the snow deeper and the temperature lower. The citizens had overcome their fascination with the unusual weather and scurried inside to the nearest wood-burning stove. The only sign of activity was up the street, where people were going in and out of Harris Mercantile, stocking up on provisions.

No one was in the doctor's waiting room, nor was Miller attending a patient in the adjacent surgery. York called out and Doc yelled back to join him in his private quarters beyond. These consisted of a sitting room, a small kitchen, the physician's bedroom, and a spare room that was spare in every sense, as there was nothing in it but a metal bed and a dresser with a basin and pitcher.

Jonathan P. Tulley, in a white hospital-style

gown, was under the covers, head on a fat feather pillow. He looked pale and weak, but was clearly alive.

So much so that, seeing York enter with the doctor, Tulley got excited and started to sit up.

"Stop that," Miller ordered, and hustled over to hold the skinny patient down. This took not much effort.

"Sheriff," the deputy said, "ye must find and capture and *hang* him!"

York came over and stood beside Tulley, who relaxed his body, though his white-bearded face remained a contorted mask. Still, the doctor was able to let loose of his charge.

With half a smile, York said softly, "Anyone in particular I should find, capture and hang, Tulley?"

"Why, the bastard what shot me!" Tulley frowned and shook his head — a little. More effort than that seemed unlikely. "But I don't envy ye, Caleb York."

York sat on the edge of the bed and springs squeaked like tortured mice. "Why's that, Tulley?"

"Wal, sir, I made my share of enemies in my time. There's a feller that accused me of jumpin' his claim. There's another that accused me of jumpin' his woman. Why,

79

there's a whole passel of such wrong 'uns out there what wrongly think I wronged 'em."

York filled in the rest of the smile. "Hate to disappoint you, Deputy. But I believe *I* was the target."

Tulley managed to rear back. "Wal, that would mean this son of a bee is the worst danged shot in the Territory. You were inside the Victory, and I was out!"

"Yes, you were outside" — York gestured to his black frock coat — "wearing this. Of mine."

". . . Oh."

York nodded.

"So ye have, over time," Tulley said, reflectively, "gathered yore own passel of enemies, then."

"I have."

"Probably a mite more than I."

"A mite."

York filled his deputy in about Burnham and the three men who appeared to be riding with him, and that they had been in Bliss Maxwell's company.

Tulley began to sit up again, and Doc scolded him and eased him back down.

But the patient said impatiently, "Make this sawbones let *loose* of me, Caleb York! You cain't go gunnin' for four men without me and my scattergun at yore side or behind ye or somewheres close and handy. . . . Say, uh . . . do I be dyin'?"

This last was aimed at Doc Miller, who said, "No. You will be in this bed for a good week, however, and there will be no gallivanting after outlaws."

"But, Doc . . . I fear the end is near. . . . I am so dang *cold.* . . ."

Miller pointed toward the window behind Tulley at his right — it was frosted over in a filigree design revealing the fine hand of Mother Nature. "There's a blizzard going on out there, Mr. Tulley. I will find you some blankets."

Tulley smiled, displaying far more teeth than one might expect. "That is the best medicine ye could perspire."

And fell asleep.

Miller came over and took York by the elbow and guided him through the apartment out into the office area. They faced each other.

"He seems lucid enough," York said.

"That's your idea of lucid?"

"For Tulley it is. Will he be all right?"

Doc nodded. "I believe so. But he's weak. Lost some blood, as you well know. Those men you mentioned — this Burnham character? You feel sure they did this?"

"Sure enough to look into it good and hard."

Doc shook his head. "You can't think Bliss Maxwell is any part of it. He's obviously a respectable citizen."

"Maybe he wasn't always."

Miller put a hand on York's shoulder. "Many a respectable man in the Southwest was a rogue elsewhere. That's the good thing about this hard country — a body can start over." He shrugged. "He may have known Burnham and those three in another life."

York buttoned his coat. "You're probably right. And Burnham likely rode out before this snowstorm got a chance to build into a blizzard. I'll check the livery and see."

York did that.

Lem Hansen, the blacksmith who owned the stable, said the four men had kept their horses with him and stayed there themselves, sleeping on straw in a stall. They had ridden out last night, around eleven, and were long gone.

Eleven p.m. — not long after Tulley was shot.

At the Victory, York had a beer at a table where he sat with Rita and filled her in on his day since he'd last seen her.

Her dark eyes had sparkle even when she

frowned. "What do you make of it, Caleb?"

"I would guess they were passing through," he said. "Probably after pulling a job somewhere, on their way to Mexico. They made a stop here, Burnham saw me — or knew this was my town — and took the opportunity to settle a score."

She gestured with an open hand. "So Tulley took the bullets meant for you, and now you . . . what? Just write it off to bad luck?"

York heaved a sigh. "For now it's all I *can* do. If they did pull a job — robbed a stage, a bank, even a train — I'll be able to confirm as much soon enough. Then when Tulley's up and around, I'll take a little time off."

Her smile was a wicked little thing making one dimple in a pretty cheek. "And take a little sojourn to Mexico?"

He nodded. "And in the meantime, ride out this storm and see who among the citizenry of our fair little town might need help. It's what they pay me for."

Getting even for what Burnham and his boys almost surely did to Tulley would be free of charge.

CHAPTER FOUR

Lucas Burnham admired Captain William Clarke Quantrill to this day. Never had he known a more natural leader of men. Never had he seen a warrior more fearless and willing to meet war on its own terrible terms.

The stories about Quantrill that were still bandied about seemed, to Burnham, preposterous. That such a man had tortured animals as a boy, skinning cats and making pigs squeal by putting bullets in them?

Twaddle.

That the adult Quantrill's idea of impressing women was to boast of hanging men from trees, several to a sturdy limb at one time?

Nonsense.

That the captain was nothing but a bloodthirsty fiend who killed and plundered for himself, not the Cause?

Shameless exaggeration.

84

Hadn't William Quantrill been a beloved schoolteacher before the war? Hadn't Quantrill gone on to lead many a Confederate officer who outranked him but were honored to serve under the great man on his now fabled raids?

Yet there were those, even now, who said some among the captain's men hated and feared him, and while the latter was true in its way, hadn't Quantrill battled superior forces over which he won many celebrated victories?

Burnham himself had been a Kansas farm boy whose father only dreamed of owning slaves, a dream the boy shared, fueled by thoughts of looting Yankees to make possible a prosperous postwar life awaiting him somewhere in a South that was but a fuzzy myth in his mind. He saw himself wearing a plantation hat and rocking on a porch with a mint julep while his chattel toiled in a field growing nothing specific.

Quantrill was already making a name when sixteen-year-old Burnham joined the band of guerilla raiders, whose captain headed up what had been a ragtag band of a dozen men that had grown to a force of over one hundred. Their leader, frustrated by the Confederate military's shameful hesitance to wage total war against Union forces, had taken it upon himself to raid Union camps, sack settlements, attack Yankee patrols, and even bring down boats on the Missouri River.

Burnham was one of many civilians among the marauders, though regular soldiers rode with them, too. Not that those riding out of uniform were of a lesser breed. The young man rubbed shoulders with the likes of the James boys and the Younger brothers, all of whom honed their special skills under the captain's leadership.

Young Luke's first taste of the Quantrill strategy of all-out war came with the raid on Shawnee, Kansas, where the boy participated in burning out the settlement. A dozen or so were slain in the attack, and Luke was responsible for two of those kills. He had felt nothing but exhilaration, that and a glow almost as warm as the orange-and-blue flames he'd helped light.

When Captain Quantrill was denied a regular command, due to the traitorous talk of his supposed bloodthirsty ways, the Union struck out at him and his men by denying prisoner-of-war status to any raider who might be captured, labeling Quantrill's men as self-serving thieves and cold-blooded killers. When had war become some kind of sissified gentlemen's game?

The captain had responded in kind, dealing death to any Unionites who surrendered, soldier or civilian alike. This raised the ire of a Yankee brigadier general, who announced that any person giving comfort and aid to the "bushwackers" would be imprisoned — women and children included. The general had figured this would drive the guerillas out of the Missouri-Kansas border area.

Part of this anti-Quantrill effort included federal troops locking up Confederate-sympathizing families in a big, badly run-down building in Kansas City, Missouri, in an attempt to cut the Rebels off from food and shelter. Perhaps that might have paid off . . . if the three-story ramshackle structure hadn't fallen down like London Bridge.

Five women died in that collapsing building, and many others, children among them, were injured terribly. A good number of these innocents were relatives of Quantrill's raiders, including the Younger brothers themselves.

The captain's vengeance came swift and unforgiving.

Quantrill and his band, now numbering four-hundred-some — mounting a carefully planned military assault in the early morning hours — hit Lawrence, Kansas, rudely rousing its three thousand citizens from their slumber. Young Luke felt honored that he was appointed leader of the fire-setting brigade by the captain himself. And whenever anyone spoke of the so-called "Lawrence Massacre," Burnham would inform them that Captain William Quantrill himself had stopped Luke from setting fire to the hotel until the guests were evacuated.

Was that the act of a bloodthirsty killer?

Far as that went, Luke didn't kill many of the cowardly civilians that day, either — though he did do in one of the first to fall, a reverend out milking his cow behind his parsonage. Homes were pillaged and plundered, stores robbed, buildings torched, and the occasional "free" black man spotted and shot (most were cowering somewhere — to him, all these black vermin were yellow).

The citizenry throughout the raid were a craven bunch, in his view — fleeing to cellars, cornfields, thickets, and ravines, some trying to swim to safety across the Kansas River. The raiders picked off many like the sitting ducks they were.

There was the occasional light moment, as when one woman and her two kiddies came out of a house that Burnham was about to set to flame. Hugging her little ones to her, she begged the raiders on horseback to leave her house standing, and claimed she was just a poor young widow woman. She was fetching enough for some fun, but, again — they were warriors, not barbarians, no matter what was said of them!

When Burnham set the house afire, it wasn't long before the supposedly dead husband came running out of the house like *he* was on fire! Then some shots rang out and the craven, lying bastard really was dead.

By sundown, the attack was over.

Tragically, one of the raiders had lost his life. But it was a fair trade, Burnham felt, as something like two hundred boys and men, who had at least had the sand to stand up for themselves, were cut down like wheat to a scythe. As darkness fell, the triumphant raiders rode to a bluff and watched the orange flames lick the sky as billowing smoke rose to add clouds to the night.

Those that considered Quantrill and his men nothing but robbers and murderers ignored the retribution from the other side that soon came down upon them and their supporters. Homes of their sympathizers were evacuated and ruthlessly looted, then burned to the ground. The time had come to leave this Missouri-Kansas no-man's land, with Texas the next stop for the raiders.

No one talked about the bravery they would show in the days ahead, and the good they would do. There was what some called the Barter Springs Massacre, which in Burnham's mind was really a battle that had their band of four hundred reducing a Union general's escort of one hundred to a mere twenty.

Then, at Bonham, Texas, at General McCulloch's direction, they'd been sent after conscription dodgers and chicken-hearted deserters, bringing some back, dispatching the rest with the kind of mercy such cowards deserved, which was none at all. The general sent the raiders to do the same with some of those uncivilized savages, the Comanches, but they proved too devious to be brought to justice.

Around then, the captain's lieutenant broke away and went off with his own band, and meanwhile Quantrill himself fell out with McCulloch, who objected to an assassination plot against a Confederate general — didn't these fools know this was war?

Suddenly some three hundred Confederate regulars were pursuing the raiders, who made it across the Red River and got resupplied as Confederate troops themselves, at a fort where nobody knew the guerillas were wanted men. After this, they made the long trek back to Missouri, pausing only for looting and burning.

Through it all, Burnham stuck by the captain. Luke never was a regular soldier, but like a lot of the raiders, he wore a gray uniform jacket, taken from the body of an actual Confederate soldier who'd been riding with the raiders; whenever one of these got themselves killed, a raider would help himself to Confederate gray.

Burnham to this day wore the jacket he'd acquired off the body of the only raider killed at Lawrence, a soldier. It was in good shape, too, as its prior wearer had got himself shot in the head. Went right through him, damn near between the eyes, so no gore or nothing got on the gray.

Things kind of fell apart after a while, and there were some that stopped believing in the captain. "Bloody Bill" Anderson, a mean son of a bitch as the necklace of Yankee scalps he wore attested, broke off a bunch of the boys. Another faction was led by George Todd, a Quantrill lieutenant, who'd even got himself elected by the men over the captain.

Things had got that bad.

But Burnham had been part of the remaining company of raiders who Quantrill assembled, intending to ride right into Washington, D.C., and kill that damn traitorous President Lincoln. Only they had to turn back when the Union forces east of the Mississippi, amassed like they were, made the plan impractical.

So they had gone back to raiding.

One such raid, in Taylorsville, Kentucky, went off the rails. With their ranks reduced to thirty or so, the guerillas were waylaid by Union irregulars, and though the captain and his men fought valiantly, a bullet took William Quantrill down when the cowards (some not in uniform) cornered him in a barn. The bullet traveled through the captain's spine, but he did not die right away. Summer of '65 it was, when William Quantrill passed away in the military prison at Louisville.

A great man taken too soon, Burnham had felt, and always would.

For a time he rode with Archie Clement's splinter group of raiders, keeping up the good fight after the official fighting was over, all through '66. But pretty soon the raiders — like Jesse and Frank James, and the Younger brothers — took the skills they'd honed under the captain and carried them over into the outlaw life.

Luke Burnham was one of those.

He had started small, as a road agent, stopping riders and demanding their money and valuables. Worked his way up to stagecoach holdups, which he got very good at, and put together his own gang of half a dozen men. They had pulled several bank jobs, and were planning a train robbery, when Wells Fargo detective Caleb York took to their trail. That had been a humiliating turn of events, as York had caught Luke in bed in a Kansas City brothel with a colored girl.

"What would your precious Quantrill say," York had wondered aloud, pressing the nose of his .44 Colt into the throat of the naked-in-bed Burnham, "if he knew you were giving money to a dusky jewel like this?"

Burnham had told the Wells Fargo man where he could go, and the Wells Fargo man had replied by cuffing him a good one with the .44. When Burnham woke up, he was in shackles in his long-johns, and that was the way York took him in.

One day York would die for that.

But the ex-Wells Fargo man, current sheriff of Trinidad, New Mexico, had not died the night before, as had been intended. Burnham and his boys had learned as much at the livery stable, when the blacksmith who ran it told them about it, just making conversation. Seemed York's deputy had been wearing Caleb's coat and got mistook for his boss.

Burnham, who had fired the shots, had no one to blame but himself for that. Perhaps, after the day's work, when they rode back to Trinidad, he could rectify his mistake.

The thirty-some-mile trek from Trinidad to Las Vegas, on horseback, had taken them all night. The weather had turned cold enough and the snowfall picked up enough that even with their Missouri Fox Trotters, known for distance, the riders arrived well after sunup. Their canvas dusters had done a fair job keeping out the chill, but Burnham and his boys were happy to drop their mounts off at the stable, where he'd arranged things in advance.

They headed to the posh Plaza Hotel, where their two rooms were a real step up from sleeping in a stable stall back in Trinidad. Two to a bed, they snored the morning away in crisp sheets and plenty of woolen blankets.

The city was blanketed, too, by the time they arose around noon, but in heavy white, the snow coming down steady — wet, heavy stuff that turned the modern little city into a wintry ghost town.

And despite the current lack of activity, Las Vegas was indeed modern, making Trinidad and so many other desert bumps in the road seem like relics of an increasingly fading yesterday. Nestled where the end of the Sangre de Cristo Mountains met the start of the Great Plains, the town had a telephone company and waterworks, and a busy train yard just east of the Gallinas River. Residential sections were chock-a-block with Victorian homes that shouted money, echoed by a thriving commercial district where two- and three-story brick buildings loomed everywhere you looked. Hell, you had to go to Denver or Tucson or El Paso to rival the place.

The amount of business here, cattle in particular, was why the Bank of Las Vegas was said to keep so much cash on hand to meet weekly payrolls.

The four men — three in their black suits, with Burnham out of place in his customary gray Rebel jacket — sat in the dining room of the Plaza. They were among the few wearing gun belts, another sign of how civilized the town had become, when not long ago Doc Holliday, Jesse James, and Billy the Kid had been welcome. The grill bustled with business — it was lunch hour, after all — at odds with the street out the windows where only a hardy few walked against the wind and driving snow.

Moody Bender was his usual gloomy self, talking between gulps of coffee. "I say we call it off. How the hell do we fight this weather?"

As if to underscore Moody's point, the wind past the windows howled.

"Can't last forever," Ned Sivley said. Then the gray little scarecrow coughed into his napkin and bloodied it some, before adding, "We can wait it out. Hotel like this ain't a bad place to do it."

"Not bad at all," Jake Warlow said. The handsome bounder was grinning lasciviously, watching a pretty waitress go by with a steaming dish in hand.

Burnham knew they couldn't afford even another day in a palace like this, but all he said over the clank of china and silverware was "No."

"No?"

"No?"

"No?"

"No," Burnham said. "We use this to our benefit."

None of his boys had been military men, Burnham knew, so the obvious strategic advantages of the situation were lost on them.

But at least now he had Warlow's attention. The cleanshaven ladies' man said, "How is a blizzard a goddamn benefit?"

"We'll be riding out ahead of it. Anyway, who's to say it's a blizzard? Snow like this don't last long in these parts."

Moody said, "Those damn horses was half dead and nose-froze when we got here."

Burnham turned over a hand, lifting his coffee cup for a sip with the other. "And they had all morning to thaw out and rest up. Anyway, you can't stop those Trotters. They just keep a-goin'."

Warlow, looking at another pretty waitress, who gave him a practiced sincere smile, said, "So you figure we can get back to Trinidad before the snow catches up with us."

"Or this downfall peters out," Burnham said, shrugging. "Look out the windows."

The dining room was warm enough that frost only edged the glass, giving a good view of the white, unwelcoming world out there, its underpopulated nature evident.

"You really think," Burnham asked, "there will be many customers at the bank today?"

"Not likely," Moody admitted. "Everybody but us would have more sense."

Burnham smirked back at him. "Why, would you rather make our withdrawal with an audience of spooked civilians lookin' on? Men who might decide to play hero, women to get all hysterical, little ones that'd start cryin'?" He was almost whispering now. "Or would you rather walk in where the bank is enjoying a dull day as lazy as a summer afternoon?"

Sivley coughed into his red-spotted napkin again, then nodded toward the frost-edged windows. "That ain't no summer afternoon out there, Luke."

"No. But it's every damn bit as lazy."

No further argument ensued. The boys knew not to question their boss too hard or he might lose his temper. They used to be five, this little gang, until Burnham shot dead that mouthy son of a bitch, Lon Dooley.

Anyway, a nice warm meal had arrived, the Blue Plate Special — roast beef, whipped potatoes, and asparagus. Perfect for cold weather, and fine fuel for the job ahead.

Before long, the Burnham bunch had checked out of the hotel and, gun belts under dusters, headed through the wet, near-blinding snowfall. They might have been hiking a snowy mountain path for all the citizens they encountered.

The Bank of Las Vegas was in the middle

of a block on the plaza — banks almost always had a building to either side of them, leaving only the front and back exposed, often situated in the middle of town. That was one reason why bank robberies were more rare in the West than the dime novelists thought — but an experienced raider like Luke Burnham was happy to be the exception.

When Burnham tried the double front doors, he found them locked, though the hours painted on the glass indicated the bank should be open. A week before, he had cased the place, and taken stock of its security measures and the number of employees, and knew what to expect under normal circumstances.

That the bank might have closed due to the weather was a possibility he'd considered. Through the building's frosted-over windows, the quartet could see only lamp glow, but that was enough to say that someone was in there, and they shared nods to that effect.

With his gloved left hand — his right was gloveless and stuffed into the slit of his duster, giving him easy access to his Colt Lightning .32-20 — Burnham pounded his fist on the door, rattling it.

Nothing.

He did the same again, and still no response.

Glancing at his boys, all of whom were frowning, concern growing that Mother Nature had upended their plans, the outlaw leader kept pounding.

Then came the scrape and click of the door unlocking, cracking open to reveal a distinguished-looking gent with white hair and white muttonchops, who Burnham recognized from his scouting as the bank president.

"I'm sorry, gentlemen," the banker said, in a deep, mellifluous voice. He was about fifty, tall and slim, and wore a tailored brown sack suit with a wingtip collar and four-in-hand tie. "Due to the lack of business, and the unfortunate weather conditions, we've closed early, I'm afraid."

"Sir," Burnham said, firm but pleasant, his hat tugged down to conceal the milky eye that might be disconcerting, "we have a sizable deposit to make."

The bank president shook his head, shrugged. "I'm sorry. I fear my staff has gone home."

Good news.

Burnham, his foot in the door, said, "We're surveyors for the Santa Fe. Been working down Trinidad way — this new spur going in?"

"Yes, well . . ."

"Finished our work and we don't want to walk around with this kind of money on our persons. Could you put it in your safe? Give us a receipt? We can make a formal deposit when you're open for business." Burnham smiled. "Storm can't last forever."

The banker thought about it. He sighed, nodded, opened the door wider. The four "surveyors" stepped inside, Moody the last in and shutting the door behind them.

Hurricane-lamp chandeliers cast a yellowish glow on the surprisingly modest facility, although the floor was marble and the usual gleaming brass touches were here and there. Three openings in a metal, fence-like framework atop a polished wooden counter served as teller windows, while a massive safe stood against the back wall, its four-inch-thick door open to reveal stacks of money below and small sacks of coin on shelving above.

An open safe like this was a common practice in the West, meant to reassure customers their money was still on the premises, and well-protected in a safe that would shut tight after closing.

The only other employee, besides the banker himself, was a security guard in a blue uniform with a blue cap, apparel that was obviously meant to suggest a police presence, but only made Burnham think of a Union soldier. The guard was a big, stupid-looking man with a handgun on his hip; he wore a mustache and suspicion, the latter manifested by resting the heel of his hand on the butt of the holstered weapon.

The bank president gestured to a desk behind a wooden spindle rail with a gate. A tall, wide, metal cabinet with short, wide drawers for maps, blueprints, or other oversize official documents hugged the wall. This area apparently served as his office.

"How much cash are we talking, gentlemen?" the banker asked, as he held open the gate door graciously, gesturing for them to join him. Only Burnham went in.

"All of it," the outlaw leader said.

The banker smiled. "Well, of course, but could you be more specific? Tell me what your count is, for your combined pay, and I will verify it."

"Certainly," Burnham said, and he turned and gave Moody a nod, and Moody — who was nearest to the guard — swung and shot him in the head.

The room was high-ceilinged enough to make the crack of Moody's Merwin spur-trigger .38 resonate. The guard, who had just enough time to form a surprised expression but not enough to go for his gun, teetered for a moment, as if he weren't already dead, then collapsed like a house of cards, landing with limbs going every which way. On the wall behind him, next to a framed hanging portrait of President Grover Cleveland, was a generous splash of red, dripping like too much carelessly applied paint.

The banker froze and the weather had not a damn thing to do with it.

"By all of the money," Burnham said, withdrawing the Colt Lighting revolver from under the duster, "I mean all of *your* money. Well, your depositors' money. Cash and coin. Do you have something we can put it in?"

Their host had turned almost as white as his head of hair and muttonchops. He remained frozen, though now looking past Burnham at the fallen guard and the blood streaming down the wall past President Cleveland's unconcerned face.

Burnham got the banker's attention by shoving the nose of the Colt into his belly, making him jump, but it did the job. And he let the man see that scarred, milky eye.

"Do you," Burnham repeated, "have something to put it in? The *money*?"

Soon the banker was kneeling at the altar

of the big safe, piling money into a canvas bag with his bank's name on it. He put the coin sacks in first, which was thoughtful, since that was where the weight should go.

But Burnham was frowning as the last banded money packets went in. "How much *is* that?"

The banker's voice, like his finger, trembled. "Current balance of our cash reserve is eighteen thousand dollars. The cash from the teller's drawers . . . which we collected from them before they left early for the day . . . brings it to just over twenty thousand."

Burnham scowled and almost spat the words: "Where's the *rest* of it?"

The banker blinked. "The rest of what?"

"The money!"

He gestured at the bag, the top limp and hanging, like a night cap. "That's all of it. That's everything."

With his left hand, Burnham grabbed the banker by his four-in-hand tie and yanked him forward until the noses of the two men almost touched. As for the nose of the Colt revolver, it was in the banker's throat, just below his Adam's apple.

Burnham's upper lip curled back. "Don't you lie to me, you greedy bastard! Everybody *knows* this bank has a hundred grand in it! Where's the rest?"

Swallowing, shaking his head, his eyes marbles of fear, the bank president said, "There *isn't* any! I can't be held responsible for rumors you've heard! People who talk about such things don't know *anything* about the reality of banking!"

"I've seen this town. It's *rolling* in it!"

"Sir," the banker said, not realizing his pandering only made Burnham more angry, "we handle most of our transactions on paper, by way of documents and ledger books. Most stores around here sell on credit, since so many of their customers have to wait for cattle sales or harvest time or till building construction is finished."

"Are you lecturing me?"

"No! Of course not."

Burnham shot him in the head.

Leaving the banker's body slumped against the now empty safe, Burnham and his boys took their leave. They were angry over the shortfall, but not as angry as the storm they now had to flee into.

CHAPTER FIVE

The ride on horseback from Trinidad to the Cullen ranch usually took twenty minutes or so.

Not today.

If he was lucky, Caleb York might make it in an hour, the road out of town an uncertain affair in a sea of white defined only by the telegraph poles that lined it, its normal straight passage compromised by drifts requiring constant small detours. Neither Caleb York nor his dappled gray gelding were accustomed to such conditions, as man and beast plowed through the kind of wind folks called a Blue Norther, with its relentless howling, swirling, blinding welcome.

Dry desert land hid under this drifting alabaster sea, but evidence to that effect was scant. Now and then, left and right of the hide-and-seek-playing road, a yucca would raise its arms in snowy surrender, and a cottonwood would stand shivering, bare but for the patchy pearly garment it wore.

York had a woolen muffler tying down his hat and knotted below his chin, his hat brim tugged down, his black coat flapping like frustrated wings. What uncovered flesh on his face remained bore a crystalline crust, and his breath was steam that mocked him, while his dappled gelding's breath from its dilated nostrils was more of the same.

York's decades in the West had found him doing many things in any number of places, but in none of them had he ever been a cowboy. He was, however, well aware of what the life of a cowpuncher entailed, from stampedes to treacherous river crossings, from torrential rain to blistering drought. Snakes, insects, brush fires, dust storms, quicksand, mud holes, and thunderstorms — none of it appealed, even to a gunfighter whose legend made a target of him. But, hell — more cowhands were killed by lightning than shootists by gunfire.

And now the cowboys of the Cullen ranch were out here somewhere in this swirling white death trying not to get frostbite or pick up pneumonia or just plain die, all to protect the rancher's precious cows — to keep the beeves moving and not just standing there stupidly to freeze, as the dumb critters were prone to do, or pile up over fences or in a gully.

What kind of fool would be out in such weather, anyway?

Of course he knew damn well what kind of fool, because he was one of them, his concern for Willa Cullen, and what she was facing in these disastrous conditions, having sent him out here. And he couldn't be sure he could even find his way to his objective through this wall of white.

Then, not far off the road, the familiar rustic log arch — with its wind-swinging, chain-hung plaque, carved with a big brash O under a firm line, the Bar-O brand — announced the sheriff's destination. He and the gelding navigated the turn, though the hard-packed dirt lane to the ranch itself soon became a guess under the treacherous beauty of snow gathered in ivory waves, like an ocean's rough waters had frozen solid.

He was just thinking he'd lost his way and was headed out onto the range to freeze and die when, like a mirage in the whirling white, the Cullen ranch revealed itself. Looking less real than a painting by your maiden aunt, two barns loomed, then emerged the rat-proof grain crib, the log bunkhouse, the nearby cookhouse with its hand pump mostly lost in snow; and the corrals at left and right, but most of all the main building, a central structure fashioned of logs Willa's late father had put up himself, with some stone add-ons. The ranch house roof was heavy with snow and silvery stuff had found its way under the overhang onto the porch, piles of it sitting on the rockers, bored misshapen spectators. But the windows burned yellow with light from kerosene lamps.

Somehow Lou Morgan, the lanky old stockman who looked after the barns, had seen York coming, and was heading out to meet him, bundled in a sheepskin coat and heavy gloves and canvas trousers, his hat tied down with a muffler, too. Morgan was walking oddly, putting one hand at a time out in front of the other. Then, approaching on the gelding, York understood: Morgan was guiding himself along a rope tied to the door of the horse barn at his back and knotted to the wood rail of the porch ahead.

This would guide the old boy from the stable to the main house and back again, without getting lost in the snow.

"Caleb York!" Morgan cried, finally recognizing the rider in the poor visibility. *"Let's get that horse in the barn!"*

York climbed down and walked his horse, following the stable man on his rope back to the barn. Soon the gelding had a stall and warmth and even hay, though this had taken up one of the few remaining berths. The barn had a wood-burning stove putting out enough heat that York wouldn't have minded curling up in a stall himself, though the wooden walls of the structure shuddered with each gust.

Morgan, spare and grizzled, his head looking almost bandaged in the cloth he'd wrapped himself in, gazed up at the visitor, pointing in the general direction of the ranch house.

"Miz Cullen will be glad to see you," Morgan said. "She's all by herself and worried to death. I don't blame her!"

York tipped his hat to the stable man and thanked him for accommodating the gelding, then headed over to the ranch house. He did not use the rope to drag himself there, as he could make out the building well enough not to, but he wouldn't be ashamed if that changed on the return trip.

York climbed the several snow-clogged stairs and got onto the porch, where fortunately no drift blocked the door. He unknotted the woolen scarf under his chin that held his hat on, and took off both the scarf and the hat. Then, after tromping snow from his boots, he knocked on the carved-wood and cut-glass door that had been purchased by Willa's late mother long before York had met either George Cullen or his daughter. He and George had been good friends, with nary a hitch, while York and Willa's relationship had been almost as stormy as this calamitous day.

He didn't have to knock twice. She jerked the door open, alarm on her pretty face, as if only more disaster could come calling about now.

When she saw who it was, she clutched York to her and squeezed him hard, an instinctive, perhaps reflexive reaction to the sight of this particular man on her doorstep at this troubled moment. She pulled him inside, then sanity returned to her, accompanied by embarrassment.

"Sorry," she said, smiling awkwardly. "It's just, uh . . . so nice to see a friendly face."

Willa Cullen was pretty without any daintiness, an almost tall young woman with an hourglass figure and creamy complexion courtesy of her late Swedish mother, who could also be credited with her daughter's straw-yellow hair, which was worn up and braided in back. At twenty-three, she was older than her years, except at those times when she was younger than them.

"I appreciate the welcome," York said, and hung up his hat and coat on hooks inside the door, which he shut behind him, reducing the roar of wind to a dull howl.

Having just hugged him, Willa — in a red-and-black plaid shirt, new-looking denims, and black leather boots — was covered in snow and general dampness herself.

"You're cold!" she said.

He jerked a thumb behind him. "It's snowing."

She formed half a smile. "I noticed."

"Now *you're* soaked."

She gestured toward the nearby living room. "There's a fire to dry us. Can you . . . stay a while?"

"If you like. I was just . . ." He looked for the right words and couldn't quite find them. So he just said, "I wanted to make sure you were all right."

Her small half smile filled itself out, but something larger was in her cornflower-blue eyes; they seemed to be watering up.

"I'm glad you're here," she said, leading him by the hand into the living room as if he were a child. "I don't know if you can help. . . . You're no cattleman."

"That I'm not." He grinned. "The only thing I know about beef is how to eat it. Maybe cook it, under pressing circumstances."

Bathed in the yellow of the window-set

kerosene lamps, the living room was a mix of her two late parents — her father's hand-hewn, bark-and-all carpentry and her mother's finely carved Spanish-style furnishings purchased on trips to Mexico. Her father's influence dominated, though — the beam ceilings, hides on the floor, mounted antlers, the stone fireplace, in which a fire fed warmth to a room that would otherwise be starving in the cold. Old rifles were wall mounted on upturned deer hoofs on either side of the fireplace.

As they neared the fire and the pair of angled rough-wood chairs draped in Indian blankets facing it, a small, wooden George Cullen – crafted table between them, she said, "You're frozen solid."

"This'll thaw me nicely," he said, nodding toward the dancing blue-and-orange flames.

They each took a chair.

Willa sat forward, hands clasped, her expression concerned. "I heard about Deputy Tulley. Is he all right?"

"Doc Miller thinks he'll recover."

She sighed. "And how is Trinidad coping with this storm?"

"Like they say at sea, the town's battened down the hatches. I took stock this afternoon, as best I could, and everyone seems to be fixed for firewood and fuel oil."

"Good. Good." She shook her head, frowning. "You should get out of those things."

"Pardon?"

"You know where my father's bedroom is?"

"No."

She told him.

"All Papa's clothes are still in there," she said, "in the armoire." She pointed to where a hallway crossed between them and the dining room. "Get into something dry before you catch your death. Can't have the legendary Caleb York dying of a cough or the sniffles."

He did as he was told. In a bedroom dominated by an old brass bed and adorned only with one hanging framed print of a herd of buffalo, he got out of his things and was standing in his red long-johns when the knock came.

He went to the door and said, "Yes?"

"Hand your clothes out. I'll put them on the hearth to dry."

"All right," he said, and did so.

When he handed the stack of clothing out, she said, "That underwear — is it damp, too?"

"Yeah."

"Get out of them. Papa's undergarments

are in the dresser. Should fit you."

Again, he did as he was told. Standing there buck naked on one side of the door, and feeling damned funny about it, he passed the clothing around and out to her. She took them with a smile and a giggle, then disappeared.

He shut the door, frowning, then glanced behind him and saw the mirror over the dresser. Well, he hoped she'd enjoyed the rear view.

From the dresser he took fresh long-johns, white ones, and black trousers and a gray shirt from the wardrobe. Everything fit him fine, which surprised him some. He'd always thought of George Cullen as a smaller man, physically, than himself. But when he thought about it, he realized that Cullen must have been good-size, merely bent over some with age. The old boy had seen his share of hard days, and was blind at the end, but always had more spine than any other two men. Three.

Dressed, including some brown woolen socks he'd found in the drawer given to underthings, York sat on the side of George Cullen's bed and thought about the dead man's daughter. They'd had a rocky time of it, Willa and Caleb. They'd expressed love for each other, early on, and had kissed more than once, though it never got much farther. She was young and he'd respected her father and, anyway, York had come to Trinidad as somebody just passing through.

Didn't seem right to have his way, then be on his way.

He'd had a job lined up with Pinkerton, in San Diego, and wanted to get shy of these old-fashioned Southwestern towns. The big city was for him. And he'd told her as much.

She had not taken it well, particularly after she'd pulled strings to get the Citizens Committee to offer him the county sheriff's job (the mayor held sway with the Territorial governor). It had gone back and forth, with him accepting the job temporarily, still intending to go, quitting, then taking it on again. Unintentionally, he'd kind of whipsawed the girl.

Eventually, with all kinds of perquisites thrown his way, he'd decided to stay, at least for a time. Only by then Willa had got herself involved with another man, a rotter, who Caleb York had come to have to kill.

It was self-defense, but tell that to the woman engaged to the rotter!

Things had settled down some between them, and they had more or less agreed to be friends, which of course was the worst thing two people who loved each other —

or at least had loved each other once — could try to pull off.

He went out there in his stocking feet and found her sitting on the hearth next to his clothes, which were laid out like a dead man.

Sitting himself in one of the rough-wood chairs, he said, "Thank you, Willa. These fit fine."

"Papa was a big man. So are you."

"Few men were ever bigger than George Cullen."

She smiled sadly. Then she looked at him and said, "I wish he were here."

"As do I."

"I mean . . . *right* here, in this situation. . . . I wish he were here."

York nodded. "Blind, your papa saw more than most."

The warmth of the fire felt very good, but the moaning, witchy cry of the wind-driven snow just outside was a reminder of reality.

"This is more than a storm," he told her quietly. "It's a full-scale blizzard. They're getting hit bad up north. Hard as we're getting it, we may be luckier than those in the other territories — Wyoming, Montana, Dakota, the rest of the Plains."

"Funny thing is," she said, eyes on the fire now, "it's last summer that set us up for this."

"How so?"

She turned to him with a smile. "You really *aren't* a cattleman, are you?"

He smiled a little, too. "No. I'm really not. I'm just a drifter trying to find his way to California. Remember?"

She laughed very softly. "I remember. . . . Do you remember how hot it got last summer?"

He nodded. "A real scorcher."

"With hardly any rain to relieve it. Streams and water holes dried up, range burned brown, feed grew short, beef prices fell. . . . We fared better than most, but our cattle were skin and bones compared to usual."

York had been aware of all that, but from a town person's perspective — cowhands coming into the Victory, needing a drink because they were "spitting cotton," merchants having to give loyal customers lines of credit.

Willa sighed, patted the thighs of her denims, and smiled at him — a smile she had to work at, though. "I would just bet you wouldn't mind if I stood you to a cup of coffee. Am I right?"

He smiled back. "Wouldn't mind at all."

She came back with two china cups brimming with coffee, handing one to him, setting the other on the rough-hewn table nearby. Then, from the other bark-wood chair, she snatched away the Indian blanket and stood with it folded over her arm, looking at him expressionlessly.

"Cold as it is," she said, "would you mind if I joined you?"

"Not at all," he said, and sipped coffee, while she slipped in beside him, covering them both with the blanket.

They sat and sipped coffee and stared at the crackling fire. Once York took it upon himself to throw another log on and stir the blaze some, then returned to their chair. Both coffee cups were empty now and resting on the table. She nestled herself next to him under the blanket, and after a while she looked up at him.

He could take a hint. He kissed her. It was gentle and sweet, but it lasted long enough to turn the corner into something else. They kissed quite a while, and he had just unbuttoned her plaid shirt, with no complaint from her, slipping his hand inside to cup a breast, when a knock at the door — loud and insistent — just about tumbled them from the chair.

Willa sat up, the blanket falling to their laps, and she quickly buttoned her shirt back up and straightened her hair absently, though it was pinned back enough not to need it.

"What could that be?" she said, and again alarm was her automatic reaction to someone at the door. She rose and, with a glance at York, said, "I'll see what it is. You just stay put."

He nodded. In his present state, staying put was the better part of valor.

Willa hurried toward the door, where the pounding was repeated before she got there. She opened it a crack, then all the way, and a snow-covered cowboy lurched in. She shut the door behind him. The cowboy stood there weaving in his duster.

"Earl," she said, gesturing to the living room, "come in and warm yourself at the fire."

"Thank you, Miz Cullen." His voice was husky and out of breath.

"I want a complete report!"

"That's what you'll get, ma'am."

York had met Earl Colson, but only once, and didn't really know the man — just that he'd been well-recommended by a rancher up north when Willa needed to hire on a new foreman.

Colson was tall for a cowboy, rail-thin, with a bony, Lincoln-esque face on which rode a handlebar mustache, currently an iced-over thing under his prominent nose. His eyes were dark blue and barely visible in slits and his eyebrows, also ice-encrusted, were shaggy caterpillars. He stumbled into the living room, still in the duster, but when York rose to offer help, the cowboy shook his head and waved that off. He fell into the other chair, drawing it even closer to the fire.

Willa had slipped away to get him a cup of coffee, which she took from a tray with refills for herself and York. She handed the new cup to her foreman, who said, "Many thanks, ma'am."

York sat on the edge of his chair, turned toward the man, whose face was frozen with something that, despite the circumstances, had little if anything to do with cold. The ice on his eyebrows and mustache was already melting, and it was as if everything on his face was weeping, except those dark blue eyes themselves.

Willa sat perched on the edge of the stone hearth, but leaving most of the fire exposed, to give her foreman the benefit of its warmth. The cowboy's stare seemed to York, at first, meant for Willa; but then Caleb realized the man's eyes were on the fire itself, almost transfixed by it.

"Hell ain't *that* color," Colson finally said,

with the barest nod at the flames. "Not orange nor red nor blue nor combinations thereof. It's white. It's the color of nothing at all."

Willa's hands held the coffee cup in her lap; her frown was so taut, her eyes almost disappeared. "What's happening out there, Earl?"

The tall cowboy swallowed. "Never seen wind the like of it . . . snow stackin' up in drifts higher than a man. And the *sleet*! Clouds of the stuff, *stingin'* you, *blindin'* you."

Colson shuddered, eyes unblinking and haunted reflected orange shimmering on his face, moisture hanging from his eyebrows and mustache.

He went on: "Horses' feet all cut to ribbons, lopin' through ice-crusted drifts. Beeves with hide and hair wore off from hoof to knee, just staggerin' along like they was drunk . . . others not even staggerin'. Just froze there solid, like statues."

Willa asked, "Are the men all right?"

Without looking at her, the foreman shrugged. "Can't rightly say. For a while they all did their best to keep them steers from piling up at fences. Finally some give up on it, got themselves sheltered as best they could in gulches and canyons. My guess? Come the thaw, we'll find a good share froze to death near their dead horses, right there where they took 'shelter.' Me, I was lucky to find my way here."

"What can I do, Earl? What can *we* do?"

"Not a damn thing, Miz Cullen." He shrugged. "Wait it out." Something like a laugh rattled out of his throat like a few coins shaken in a can. "Ridin' over here I seen the damnedest things. I been punchin' cows since just after the war, but never saw the like. Banks so deep steers're stuck in it — livin', breathin', but stuck in one spot, and sorta . . . screamin'. Like some horrible horn blowin' from someplace inside 'em! Not able to move and get themselves clear. Miz Cullen, it's so deep in some places, the cows are buried, only their horns stickin' out of the snow to mark their graves."

Willa was bent over, her hands on her face. York watched the foreman, who was staring, staring, staring at the fire.

After a while, the foreman said, "I'd take it kindly, Miz Cullen, if I could head to the bunkhouse and stretch out some. I don't think I'm helpin' out there. Not no more. And we got a good potbellied stove in there, and plenty a wood and it's a-goin'. I know, 'cause I can make out the smoke from the chimney, nice and gray and not white at all."

"Please do," Willa said with a supportive little smile.

The foreman had trouble getting to his feet and York was right there, helping him.

"Can you walk okay?" York asked.

"All them hours in the saddle," the foreman said with an embarrassed grin, "a man's feet in his boots can get froze so stiff, walkin' don't come all that easy."

"I'll help you."

York took the man in the duster by the arm and kept him upright, then leaned him against the wall. After getting back into his black frock coat and hat (again tying it down with the muffler) and gloves and boots, York opened the door and walked the foreman out into the hungry storm.

As Colson had said, gray smoke from the bunkhouse stood out in the swirling white, and that allowed York to help the foreman make it over there. Also, night had fallen, and lamplight from within the Dog House, as the cowboys' quarters were often called, stood out in the dark, not completely blotted out by the squall.

York stepped inside with him. The familiar bunkhouse bouquet of sweat, manure, chaw, unwashed socks, and smoke from coal-oil lamps greeted them. A number of other cowboys were already under blankets in their bunks or huddled around the potbellied stove. Their faces looked damn near as white as the world outside, their eyes wide and unblinking, shrouded in shock. But it was warm in there, considering.

The foreman said, "Thank you, Sheriff."

"You need to do something for that frostbite."

"I'll get an Irish potato from the cookhouse," Colson said.

"What for?"

"You scrape it raw and rub it on your fingers and feet and ears. Be fine."

York didn't have any better advice, although he wondered, the next time he saw Colson, whether the foreman would have any of those appendages left.

Within fifteen minutes, York and Willa were again together in their chair in the fireplace warmth. She was snuggled close, but her words weren't of love.

"It will never be the same," she said.

"The cattle business?"

She nodded. "The Bar-O. We'll need to have more feed for the cattle in winter. We'll need more fencing, to rotate pastures, and grow plenty of hay. Seems crazy to say it, but we have too much land. We need smaller herds. We need to be" — she sighed — "not just ranchers, but farmers."

"You think a man like Colson will trade his rifle and pony for a pitchfork?"

She laughed a little. "Does sound unlikely. How about you, Caleb? Care to turn in your badge and six-gun for a posthole digger?"

They sat and stared at the crackling, snapping fire.

"This blizzard won't last forever," York said, "and like I said before — we're not getting the worst of it here."

"It's bad enough."

"It surely is. And your cattle were in better shape than many, when the snow came. The future will come, too, like it always does, and we'll deal with it."

She was looking at him now. "Together?"

"Is that what you want?"

"Well . . . I don't know that I want you heading back to town, after dark, in this blizzard."

He shrugged. "I know where your father's bedroom is. I could camp out there. That'd be most hospitable of you."

She slipped out of the chair and stood before him, back to the fireplace. She was in relative darkness but the edges of her were fiery. One by one, she unbuttoned the plaid shirt. Then she undid her belt and undid the denims and let them drop to the floor. She stepped from them . . .

. . . a woman in red long-johns and low-riding cowboy boots.

York was smiling, laughing a little.

He stood. Stripped down to his long-johns while she stood on one leg at a time and pulled off first one, then the other boot.

"Two fools," he said, "in their union suits."

Her hands were on her hips. Yet, covered neck to ankle, she was in a way naked, every curve showing, every peaked hill, every lush valley.

Rather shyly, she said, "It's only right I tell you."

"Tell me what?"

". . . I'm not a virgin."

York shrugged. "Neither am I."

He smiled and she smiled.

"Do you know where my bedroom is?" she asked.

"No," he said.

"I'll show you."

She held her hand out to him, and did.

Most hospitable indeed.

CHAPTER SIX

Luke Burnham and his boys went from the bank they'd robbed — and the men they'd killed — to the stable where their horses waited, which, thanks to Burnham's careful planning, was an easy walk even in the falling, gathering snow.

In the stalls, out of the stable man's view, they transferred the money from the canvas bank bag into their saddlebags. They did not count their take, just divided it up so that it would fit in four saddlebags, with the coin distributed evenly as to weight.

Their Missouri Fox Trotters were fed and rested; the only sign of the ordeal of the ride from Trinidad to Las Vegas last night was the worn-away hair on the ankles of the steeds. But the animals seemed up to the return trip, though Burnham almost envied the dumb beasts' lack of awareness of the trials that lay ahead.

The four men — dusters over their coats,

their hats tied down with woolen scarfs, looking like they were suffering terrible toothaches — rode south with the Blue Norther at their backs. Almost immediately the snowfall lessened from what they'd experienced in Las Vegas, though it remained steady. The Burnham bunch would be well shy of Las Vegas by the time any discovery was made. No one was pursuing them yet — the emptied bank and the dead banker and guard were inside a building with a CLOSED sign on the door.

No one human was pursuing them, that is. They raced against Nature, staying ahead of the blizzard that built behind them like an inferno of white, a conflagration not of fire but of ice.

And by the time the squall caught up with them, midafternoon, their pace had already slowed. Even riding single file, spaced close together, each rider would lose sight of his fellow travelers for endless, unsettling minutes at a time.

For all the dangerous raids on which Luke "Burn 'Em" Burnham had followed Captain Quantrill to hell and back, none compared to this chill peril. Burnham rode as hard as he dared, in the lead, spurring his little band on, but — within the cold cavern of his mind — he was chastising himself for mistakes too late to unmake.

He should have bought or stolen new steeds for the journey. He should never have allowed that damn lunger Sivley along, the man's coughs so frequent and hacking that they rose above the banshee wind. And of course he should have made certain that it was Caleb York he'd shot down in the street in Trinidad.

But that latter failure kept him going, kept driving himself and his steed forward. If they could make it back to Trinidad and into hiding until this goddamn storm let up, he would have his long dreamed of revenge before riding on to a life of ease in Mexico.

Time became a meaningless thing as they rode in the ever-dropping cold and the swirling snow, with its cutting sleet finding whatever exposed flesh it could, tiny bees anxious to sting. They were in limbo, in purgatory with hell at their heels, with the whistle and howl and moan around them like tortured, damned souls warning and welcoming them at once.

With no landmarks to guide them, other than the telegraph poles along the road, they had no sense of where they were, and how far — or how *not* far — they had come.

The visibility was so poor, they rode past the Brentwood Junction relay station without realizing it. There they could have bought (or stolen) fresh mounts, or just taken shelter and had the station man and his wife give them food and drink. Even in this weather, they would have been facing only an hour or so more of the torture.

But the storm, consuming them now, denied them that mercy. And Burnham was starting to think they would die out here, their money unspent, his revenge not taken, an ignominious defeat for a warrior who (in his own humble opinion) had shown such high valor and done so very much for a noble cause.

They slowed to a crawl. Sivley, in fourth position, was either coughing softer or falling even farther behind. Burnham had long since thought that the lunger needed killing, but didn't bother, because the man wasn't slowing them down. He was coming to the conclusion, though, that putting the scarecrow out of his misery would be a thing of mercy for all four of them.

And if the lunger's hacking cough grew so faint that Burnham and the others lost track of him, then Sivley's saddlebag of money would also be lost track of. Couldn't have that.

He raised a hand and yelled, *"Whoa!"* loud enough that even the whipping wind couldn't blot it out. Behind Burnham, Jake Warlow brought his horse to a stop, yelled *"Whoa!"* also, and behind him Moody Fender did the same, and Ned Sivley, weaving in his saddle, came to a halt as well.

Burnham climbed down from his animal. Moving through the eddying white, he walked past Warlow, nodding at him, then Fender, and as he looked up at Sivley, Burnham had his right glove hand through the slit pocket of the duster to rest that hand on the butt of his holstered Colt Lightning revolver.

"We're almost there, Ned," Burnham said, though of course he had no idea of where the hell they were. "You gonna make it?"

His cough an awful, lung-shredding thing, Sivley nodded. Even this close up, the lunger looked like a ghost in the swirl of snow, with only the red of his blood on the scarf wrapping his lower face giving him any color at all.

"You need to keep up, Ned," Burnham said. "If not, you get left behind. But the money won't."

"You . . . you'd kill me, Luke?"

"Wouldn't have to, Ned. This Blue Whistler of a storm would do the job, 'less you did yourself in, to stop your sufferin'. Now. *Can . . . you . . . keep . . . up?"*

132

"I can . . ." He coughed. ". . . I can, Luke. You can count on me."

Burnham had to shout to be heard, not just by Sivley but the other two. "Okay! But I want you and that animal to come around and fall in behind me! I need to keep my eye on you!"

"Yessir!"

Burnham walked Sivley's trembling, struggling Trotter by the bridle and guided the mount and its pathetic master into second position, Warlow making room.

Don't despair! Burnham yelled to his men. *We* have *to be close to Trinidad!*

But of course he had no real idea if that were true.

And, ironically, it was Burnham's own horse that brought things to a head. The animal began to weave, and as it went over sideways, landing hard and sending up a powdery blast of white, Burnham managed to slip off the animal in the opposite direction. He stood standing in what, if the telegraph poles could be trusted, was the middle of the road.

The rest of the little group had jerked their horses to a halt, and now Burnham looked up at the mounted Sivley, contemplating shooting him and stepping up into his saddle, when the lunger's horse collapsed as well. Somehow Sivley, perhaps having seen what had happened with Burnham and his ride, managed to slip off on the opposite side, too. Otherwise he would have had a leg crushed under the heavy steed.

Burnham examined both his horse and Sivley's, assuming he would have to put a merciful bullet in the head of each. But both animals were already dead, their snouts covered in ice crystals, their eyes cold, wide-open marbles. Even a dumb beast, it seemed, could feel terror.

Suddenly Sivley was beside him. "What do we do now, Luke? Ride two to a horse?"

Burnham was thinking, but it didn't take long to realize he would have to kill Sivley and then take out one of his two boys — he'd make it Moody, because of the man's sour attitude — and then he and second-in-command Warlow would take the surviving mounts. After transferring the money from the saddlebags of the dead animals to those of the two live ones, they would ride on alone. Yes. That was the best plan of action.

Then Warlow's animal collapsed, and he too managed to hop off.

"*Hell!*" the outlaw shouted.

That left Fender the only man still on horseback, with three other men standing knee-deep in the white that had a road under it. Fender's right hand with a gun in it came out quick, and then Burnham's gun was out, too — both had settled a hand on their gun butts under their dusters when this fuss over horses began, thanks to the damn horses themselves dying on them.

It seemed like a long time, but was only a few seconds before Fender's animal — perhaps reacting to what the other Trotters had done — also collapsed on his side, with Moody awkwardly slipping off.

Burnham went over. This horse was still breathing, but obviously useless. He shot it in the head. The snow cut off the sound of the report like a hand going over a scream.

Now, in an awkward row, lay four dead horses, with four men just standing there looking down at them as motionless as the flurries surrounding them were not.

As motionless as the dead beasts themselves.

Another few seconds dragged by, and the outlaw leader said, "Saddles and saddlebags. We walk the rest of the way."

They did walk, each with a saddle over his back and saddlebags over an arm. With the telegraph poles to guide them, they walked. Night fell, though they barely noticed. What seemed an eternity passed before they abandoned their saddles but still clung to their money-stuffed saddlebags.

Burnham's eyes stayed on the horizon, where he hoped Trinidad would present itself, perhaps by way of lamps on in the windows of buildings. No sign of that. The eternity they experienced lasted less than an hour, but what an awful hour it was.

They were walking side by side now, like the Earps and Doc Holliday heading for their showdown with the Clantons, but not looking nearly as menacing. Washed in white, coated in ice, they walked. The storm had beaten these boys like whipped puppies, and they shambled along pitifully, skirting drifts, but seldom in snow any less deep than to their knees.

But Burnham was impressed that Sivley hadn't given in to the storm. All of these men were having thoughts of curling up in the snow and just sleeping a while, just get a little rest before moving on . . . and had they done that, of course, they really *would* have moved on. . . .

Burnham was in the best shape of this bad lot — bad men in a bad way — and was the first to hear the squeak and rattle rise over the wind.

He put a hand on Warlow's shoulder and said, *"Listen!"*

The sound became less abstract, revealing itself as a buckboard approaching from behind them, the wheels and reins making a slow but distinctive rhythm.

The four outlaws turned and stood and watched the buckboard emerge from the swirling white, like a mirage on wheels. A man in a wool-lined sheepskin coat, his hat tied under his chin just as Burnham and his boys had theirs, was driving two horses that looked fresh, considering the circumstances, gray Vs of steam curling from their nostrils. The beasts even had some whinnying left in them.

Next to the driver sat a boy of perhaps twelve, similarly attired. Neither had their faces covered, their cheeks bright red.

The driver slowed the horses to a halt, then called, "Hop in back, you men!" He was husky and in his thirties. "My son and I saw your dead animals back there! Damn shame."

"We were headed for Trinidad," Burnham said.

"You're almost there. Five mile or so. My name is Horton, John Horton. I have a small ranch near here. We're heading into town to get supplies while we still can. This blizzard is going to last a while. Ever see anything its like?"

137

"Can't say I have," Burnham said.

The rancher gestured behind him. "Got an empty wagon here. You boys climb in now. We'll get you somewhere safe and warm. . . . You need help with that one feller?"

Sivley was only barely conscious, and stopping like this had only made it worse. Warlow was steadying the weaving man by an arm.

"No, thanks," Burnham said. "We can manage."

"Well, we're glad to help," the rancher said, and Burnham shot him in the face.

Scarlet blossomed in the white, then wilted to nothing. Next to the man, the boy's eyes grew big and the lad sat there frozen, not with cold but with fear and surprise as his father slumped over, almost falling from the buckboard. A rifle between the dead father and the boy just leaned there, doing nobody any good. The son didn't even think to reach for it when Warlow shot him, twice, both times in the head. Scarlet again blossomed briefly.

Father and son were awkwardly hugging now, doing a decent job of it, considering they were dead men.

Burnham said to Warlow, "You and Jake get them down from there. Drag 'em away from the road a mite. I'll get Ned in back."

The outlaw leader helped his frail follower up and into the buckboard, empty of anything but a tarpaulin, with which Burnham covered him. Killing the lunger would have been possible, and profitable, but the raider was enough of a military man not to leave the wounded behind. He had certain principles.

Fender rode in back with Sivley, who was unconscious, and covered himself some with the tarp, too. All the saddlebags of money were stowed back there, as well. Pity to lose the saddles.

Warlow took the reins and Burnham helped himself to the rifle.

In half an hour they were in Trinidad.

By nightfall, Bliss Maxwell was fairly certain that Lucas Burnham and his little gang would not show.

The pleasant-featured merchant, with his prematurely gray hair, was seated on a sofa in the sitting room of his quarters above the Maxwell Boots, Saddle, and Harness Depot. He wore his suit, though not his tie, staying warmly clad as even with his coal stove doing its considerable best, the cold outside was finding cracks through which to squeeze.

A kitchen (with that stove) was adjacent through a wide archway; a short hallway led to a pair of bedrooms. The apartment boasted comfortable chairs, a settee, several framed landscapes in oil, and a reading lamp on a table by the sofa, the lamp affixed by a tube to the gas chandelier (he was in the middle of *Ben-Hur* by Lew Wallace, former governor of New Mexico Territory). The pink-and-light-blue floral wallpaper provided a cozy gentility that took some of the edge off the hoarse cry of the storm rattling the windows at his back.

The apartment's furnishings — dark wood with cushions, its carpet a large Oriental — were all reflective of the status Bliss Maxwell had achieved in Santa Fe, before competition forced him to sell his general store. The fine things around him were a reminder of what he'd had in the past, and an inspiration for what he intended to have in the future.

He was dating the local preacher's pretty daughter and hoped a real dwelling, not just an apartment, would soon house his things and her.

With so many good possibilities in the offing, Maxwell had been reluctant to be party to the scheme his old gang leader, Luke Burnham, had proposed in the cantina two days before. He had no moral objections to the Las Vegas bank robbery, and would not have been surprised to learn two men had been murdered in its commission. Nor would the father-and-son Samaritans killed on the snow-choked road to Trinidad have come as a shock.

How could he have been surprised or shocked, having ridden with "Burn 'Em" Burnham for two years?

But Maxwell would have preferred not to risk his new identity and his respectable reputation on some reckless criminal enterprise.

No — that wasn't a fair way to put it — Burnham was a careful planner, nothing reckless about his crooked ways. The problem was the outlaw's ruthless disregard for the lives of others. That kind of thing could bring down the law on them.

Of course, Maxwell should be safe enough. He had, after all, played no role in the robbery. He had merely collected provisions, as instructed by Burnham, to prepare for the four outlaws to hole up in this apartment until the storm blew over and the heat from the law died down. He *was* troubled that Burnham had expressed a desire for taking revenge upon Caleb York while in Trinidad.

But what did that have to do with Bliss Maxwell?

And if any of this came to light, he could claim to have been a hostage, not an accomplice.

Still, as the day turned into night, Maxwell assumed the enormity, the severity of this freak storm had swallowed up the Burnham gang. Either they'd encountered conditions in Las Vegas that made carrying out their plan impossible or at least unwise, or they had gone through with it and ridden for Trinidad despite the hazard.

And, in this case, they had run into a hellish blizzard that had likely frozen them dead somewhere between here and Las Vegas.

He laughed humorlessly. What kind of horses on God's earth could have endured what Burnham would have put them through? An all-night ride to Las Vegas in snowfall that threatened to become a storm? And then an all-day ride back to Trinidad in the midst of the deadly threat that storm had carried out?

Absurd.

If they'd been dumb enough to do that, "Burn 'Em" Burnham had finally bitten off more than he, and his little crew, could chew.

And frankly Bliss Maxwell would shed no

tears over that. Yes, he could have used his share of a hundred-thousand-dollar take. Who couldn't? But he still felt confident that when the railroad spur came in, the market for the saddles that his man Juan Salazar made, and the harnesses he himself skillfully fashioned, would make him one of the wealthiest and most respected merchants in town.

In the Territory!

Right now, however, demand for his wares was modest. Many in Trinidad couldn't afford a horse — a work animal cost a hundred fifty, and you had to add another fifty dollars for a decent saddle horse. Saddles themselves cost thirty dollars for a functional model, and sixty or more for the fancy hand-tooled ones.

But as Trinidad grew, and became a railhead with swells stopping for a while, spending big, and cowboys passing through, wages burning a hole? Why, those saddles would almost ride out of his shop on their own. And the harnesses would shake themselves on the way out the door.

Still, his savings from the sale of his general store were wearing thin. So the Las Vegas bank haul would have been a blessing, no question. Trouble was, having Luke Burnham in your life, even temporarily, was a risky proposition.

Nonetheless, Bliss Maxwell had done what his old outlaw leader had asked of him. For one thing, he'd gotten his saddle maker out of the way, telling the little Mexican to take some time out to visit family and friends in Chihuahua. "After this weather," Maxwell had told Juan yesterday, "we won't sell a single saddle for a month."

Juan was about forty but retained a boyish look and attitude. "You are right, Señor Maxwell. But I can add to our supply. It take time to make the fine saddle. You will have more to sell when things get better."

"No, Juan," he'd said, putting a fatherly hand on the small man's shoulder. "You have worked very hard, and for little pay. You deserve a vacation."

Finally Juan nodded, then said with a grin, "When the train comes to Trinidad, it will pay us both well, Señor Maxwell."

"I know, I know. But this snow will have to melt first, and the mud it leaves behind dry out, before work on the spur can continue."

So Maxwell had insisted, and Juan — smiling and grateful — had gone off, borrowing the boss's own horse.

And much of today had been spent with the merchant making room in the workshop behind the building, which was somewhere between a big shed and a small barn, for the horses the Burnham boys would ride here.

Would have ridden here.

No real harm had been done. He had bought several bales of hay from Lem Hansen, supposedly for his own horse, whose stall in the workshop was empty with Juan off riding the animal, though of course Lem knew nothing of that. So there would be hay on hand when Juan returned. What did that hurt? Having flour and jerky on hand wasn't a bad thing, either.

Maxwell returned to *Ben-Hur,* where the hero had just rescued his Roman captor from the sinking ship on which Judah had been a slave. Exciting reading. He had almost forgotten his own adventures and woes when a knock came at his door, off the kitchen; an exterior staircase with landing was alongside the building.

"Yes?" he said to the door. "Who is it?"

Burnham's voice growled: "Who the hell do you think? Open this damn thing, fool!"

Hell! They'd made it!

Maxwell did as he was told. Covered in icy white, the four who stumbled in might have been ghosts, bedraggled ghosts at that. Burnham came in first, followed by Jake

Warlow. Moody Fender dragged a barely conscious Ned Sivley in. They shed their dusters and unwrapped their heads from the ice-crusted mufflers that had secured their hats, all of the apparel unceremoniously dumped on the possum-belly table, along with saddlebags from each man.

Without a word, Burnham dragged chairs over from the table and set them around and facing the cast-iron coal-burning stove as if it were a campfire. In a way it was, but this campfire had several cooking and warming ovens, and a coffeepot going. The kitchen was small but modern, with a soapstone sink, copper hot-water tank, and black-tin security safe to keep foods from pests.

Warlow, Fender, and Sivley settled into chairs, but Burnham took Maxwell by the arm and walked him the few steps into the sitting room.

Whispering harshly, the outlaw leader said, "What's the sleeping setup?"

Maxwell gestured vaguely. "Two bedrooms. Accommodate two to a bed. Sofa out here — I can take that. There's a room off the shop where the Mexican sleeps, if you want privacy. I got rid of him like you said."

Burnham, who seemed muzzy, said, "I

146

didn't tell you to kill him!"

"I *didn't* kill him," Maxwell said, rearing back. "Good God, man. I sent him out of town. To spend time with his relatives south, where it isn't snowing like a bastard."

Burnham gathered himself, then put a hand on the merchant's shoulder. "You get your coat on and go out and deal with the horses. All we have is two, but they're in good shape. Hitched up to a buckboard. Left 'em by that little barn in back. You got room in there?"

Maxwell nodded. "That's our workshop. I cleared it some, made room. There are two stalls, enough for those horses. Not room enough for the buckboard, though."

Burnham sighed. "Well, get those horses inside before they freeze, too. We had four Trotters drop under us."

"I admit I'm surprised you made it under these circumstances."

"I've seen worse," Burnham said.

Both men knew that wasn't true, unless you counted the towns the raider had burned to the ground.

Maxwell bundled himself up in his frock coat and gloves, tied his derby on with a muffler, and went down to deal with the horses. Getting them unhitched and taken into the workshop, one at a time, through

147

its rear double doors and into its stalls, was a job as tedious as it was damn cold. Took him a good forty minutes.

When he returned, the outlaws had helped themselves to cups of coffee, which they had laced with rye whiskey from expensive bottles that their host had laid in, buying them from the Victory in expectation of their arrival. All but Burnham were still seated before the stove. The leader was in the nearby sitting room, on the sofa at the reading table with *Ben-Hur* pushed onto the floor. Stacks of money were before the outlaw, cash and coin, and at first it made Maxwell smile.

Then it didn't.

Slowly, the merchant settled beside the outlaw leader, who was counting the money on the reading table before him, frowning.

Maxwell asked, "How much is that?"

"Just over twenty thousand."

"So . . . that's *my* share, right?"

Burnham shook his head. "Wrong."

"You don't have to be a mathematician to know that five into one hundred thousand is twenty thousand."

Burnham's head swiveled toward Maxwell, his glowering gaze — half of which was that milky eye in its scarred setting — an unsettling thing. "And five into twenty

148

thousand is four grand."

Maxwell frowned in confusion. "You're saying . . . that's the whole *haul*?"

"This is the whole haul."

The merchant felt red rise up from his neck. "What the hell happened to that bank always keeping one hundred thousand in its safe? You had it on good authority, remember?"

The head swiveled back, and the outlaw resumed to recounting the money. "Seems I was misinformed. Some folks just like to exaggerate, I guess."

Maxwell kept his voice down as he said harshly, "So I'm putting my reputation, my damn *life*, on the line, having your rabble as house guests for God knows *how* long . . . for a lousy four thousand bucks?"

Burnham stopped counting. He folded his hands. Turned his head toward Maxwell and the milky eye seemed to stare harder than the working one. "Four thousand is a small fortune. *Not* so small, really. You rode with me, Silas."

Silas was Maxwell's real first name.

The raider went on: "You *know* the risks this life entails."

Maxwell said nothing. His insides boiled with rage, but he feared this man, and only

149

quietly said, "How long do you intend to stay?"

Burnham shrugged. "Till the storm lets up, likely. Thing like this could stop in two seconds, or two days. Or, hell — two weeks."

Maxwell closed his eyes and kept them closed for a while, as if maybe all of this would go away when he opened them. But when he did, it didn't.

"I laid in provisions," Maxwell said quietly. "And I have indoor plumbing. So you can wait this out, if your boys don't get cabin fever on me."

"They *could* get a mite restless." The outlaw leader grinned. "But I have an idea. Had plenty of time to think on that lazy ride we took to Trinidad, y'know."

Already Maxwell didn't like the sound of this. "*What* idea, Luke?"

Burnham nodded toward the windows behind them. "This town is pretty well slowed to a halt, I'd say. You agree, Silas?"

"Please don't call me that."

"Fine. Fine. But rolling into town, seems like Main Street's one big damn drift, the whole place snowed in and snowed under, and honest folks are just as holed up as we reprobates are."

"That's right. This town is as frozen over as the Purgatory River."

150

Burnham pushed the money-piled reading table away and turned to Maxwell with a smile, sitting sideways on the couch. Folded his arms. Looked at him with two eyes, only one of which saw. "Tell me about the bank."

"Tell you about . . . what *about* the bank?"

"Any idea — as a man not prone to exaggeration — what the cash on hand might be?"

"Well . . . probably at least ten thousand, maybe as much as twenty. Could be more, I suppose. You're not thinking . . ."

"Let's call it twenty. Which is better? Five shares of twenty, or five shares of forty? I'm no mathematician either, but that's eight thousand, when it's forty grand you're dibbyin'. That really *is* a fortune. Not small at all. A man could live in Mexico a long, happy time on eight thousand American dollars. And a merchant tryin' to weather tough times till things turn in his favor, that's a lot of cushion to lean back on."

"No."

"No, it isn't? Or was my cipherin' off-kilter?"

"Of course it wasn't, but I *live* here. I won't have you robbing the bank in my own town and then hiding out with me."

Burnham shrugged, gestured around

them. "We're already doing that. And four people are dead, ol' partner, on the bank robbery that you are already in on. The Las Vegas one?"

Maxwell didn't even bother to ask how the gang had managed to kill four people. Instead he said, "The money will be in the safe, and the bank won't be open for business. Do you have the wherewithal to blow that safe? No. We'll just have to settle for our small fortunes."

"Where does the bank president live?"

"Here in Trinidad, of course."

"Where in Trinidad?"

"I'm against this."

Burnham smiled. Somehow that milky eye seemed even worse hovering over a smile. A smile like that, anyway. "Silas, do you recall that upstanding gent in Lawrence who refused to tell us where to find that Jayhawker leader? And do you recall just how I went about convincin' him to share that information with me?"

"Name is Peter Godfrey. He lives on the third floor of the bank building." Maxwell shook his head. "Luke. Be reasonable. You had a hell of a day, I'm sure. You need rest so you can think straight. We should explore this idea in the morning."

"Are you saying I'm not thinking straight,

old friend?"

"No. But I *am* saying, even with this town snowed in, the law in Trinidad is still Caleb York. And that man is hell on two legs. There would be no back-shooting. He would come straight at you. You would still have *him* to deal with."

"I'm counting on that," Burnham said.

CHAPTER SEVEN

The snow had reached the bottom of the windows of the ranch house kitchen where Willa Cullen served Caleb York scrambled eggs, fried potatoes, and biscuits with honey.

York was back in the clothing that had dried overnight, having retrieved them from the hearth of a fireplace where flames were still working. Willa wore a white bib apron over a tailored dress (likely a ready-made, York figured) the color of her cornflower-blue eyes — straight-cut bodice, high collar, and tapered sleeves. No plaid shirt and denims today — was she painting a picture of the wife she might one day be to him? Had this been contrived to ensnare him? If so, when had a sprung trap felt so comfortable?

She served herself and sat down next to him at the table for four.

They ate in silence for a while, exchanging shy smiles, embarrassed but in no way ashamed. The wind was whistling at the moment, not roaring, and the snowfall seemed to have let up some. Some.

Between bites of eggs, York said, "I guess we've moved past it."

She blinked at him. "Past what?"

"The friendship stage."

She smiled a little, and he grinned.

Willa got up — was she blushing, and turning her back to him to hide it? — and took the coffeepot from the stove, then refreshed his cup.

At his shoulder, she said, "So what's next?"

"We'll both have to mull that. I'm no rancher, and you aren't cut out for town. So for now . . ."

She leaned in and nibbled at his ear. "Very good friends?"

"Real damn good," he admitted.

She went back to her chair. "I may not *have* a ranch after this."

He shook his head. "You'll have a ranch. Like you were saying last night, the going may be different, here on out. But it'd take a lot more than a little snow to bring down George Cullen's daughter."

She was smiling, picking at her scrambled eggs. "A little snow?"

He forked up some potatoes. "This is New

Mexico. There's gonna be more sun than snow, when the reckoning comes." He pushed his plate away a few inches. "Afraid I have to get back to Trinidad. Not sure what a sheriff can do to help much, when Nature gets in a mood. But I have to be available."

Her frown was of concern. "Please tell your deputy I'm thinking of him."

"I will do that."

Soon they were at the door. He had a hunch she'd be getting out of that dress that matched her eyes and into her rancher-gal plaid shirt and jeans as soon as he left, but he appreciated the trouble she'd gone to for him. Loving this young woman wasn't tough at all, and he liked that she had both a hard and soft side. A woman in this country, in such times, needed that.

"I heard coyotes last night," she said. "Sounded mean and hungry."

"There were wolves out there, too. Howling like they were tryin' to sing along with the wind."

"I heard them."

He was putting on the long black frock coat. "All manner of predators come out in weather such as this, when their prey's at its weakest. You'll lose some cattle to them. Not as many as to the cold, but . . . you *will* lose

156

some that way."

She was frowning at him, leaning around to get a better look at something at the back of the coat he'd just put on and was now buttoning up. "What *is* that? Is that blood?"

He nodded and snugged on the cavalry-pinched Stetson. "Tulley's. Should have been mine."

"I could mend those bullet holes."

He smiled. "I didn't take you for a seamstress."

She smiled. "I'm a woman. I may run this place, but I am *not* a man."

"Noticed that. No mending of this garment just yet. I want the men who almost killed Tulley to know who's come for them."

She nodded, her smile barely there . . . but there. That she understood and approved meant much to him.

They were standing close, her face tilted up, his down. They were deciding whether a good-bye kiss was called for. York decided it was and gave her a soft, gentle one. They stood there looking at each other from just a few inches, then she kissed him back, hard, forceful, passionate enough to have gotten him out of his coat and more, if he'd let it.

And she knew as much, backing away a little, her smile a pretty, pretty mischievous thing. She folded her arms over her pert bosom and watched as he tied the muffler around the hat.

"You don't look like a legend," she said, "in that torn coat and muffler knotted under your chin."

"It is deceiving," he said, touched his brim, gave her his own mischievous smile (though not at all pretty), and went outside to find his way to his horse.

The snow had trailed off enough that he didn't have to embarrass himself by using old Lou Morgan's rope getting from porch to barn. She watched from the doorway, but not for long, the cold and snow chasing her back inside, however warm her sentiment.

The dappled gelding — after a good night's sleep (York had found the animal lying flat in the stall) and well-fed on oats and straw — was ready to ride. And ride the gelding he did, all right. Not hard but steady, slowing only to navigate the drifts along the telegraph-pole-marked road, and again when York spotted the frozen legs of horses, hooves rising from snowbanks as if in surrender.

He counted four horses that had died along here last night, fairly close together, and that made York sad, easily as sad as if they had been humans. After all, people should be smart enough not to be out in this merciless cold and snow, while the horses they rode had no choice. It did not occur to him that he apparently wasn't smart enough not to be out in this weather, either.

Humans had died on this frozen byway, too, but York did not see the murdered father and son who had been dragged off the road by Burnham's boys, the snowfall since having hidden these creatures, their corpses more easily interred in the white than equines.

So when the sheriff rode into Trinidad, whose Main Street was a weirdly beautiful and still sea of white waves, he had no notion that the Luke Burnham gang was yet in town. He left the gelding at the livery stable, where there was feed and warmth and a stall for the animal, then walked over to his office.

Without Tulley tending things, the interior of the small jailhouse office was damn near as chill as the out of doors. York built a fire in the potbellied stove and then went over to the wall of wanted posters, reading them over, like a man window-shopping. His eyes lingered on the Burnham poster, which he had tacked back up after showing it around. He took it down again and tucked it folded into a pocket.

In a drawer of his desk there were more circulars, and he sat and went quickly through them. The stove hadn't kicked in yet when he got up and was about to go, then he paused and smiled. Then he went over to grab his deputy's scattergun off the gun rack before getting out of there. He would return when a climate difference could be told between inside and outside.

Doc Miller was not in, but his office was unlocked, and York was able to walk right into Tulley's sickroom, pull up a chair and sit while his deputy in a nightshirt sawed logs. This was a sound to which York was well accustomed, as Tulley often snoozed in the cell the old boy used as lodging. Previously, York had found the snoring either annoying or amusing; right now it seemed reassuring.

Tulley looked good. For Tulley. His color was fine, and he appeared no skinnier than usual, nicely warm under several blankets. With the doc and the deputy both out in their respective ways, York rose after a few minutes and leaned Tulley's shotgun against the wall by the window onto the street.

Somehow the small clunk that made was enough to nudge Tulley awake, his eyes snapping open like a man who heard a prowler, although he did not sit up. Apparently he was still too sore for that.

"Caleb York!" Tulley said, eyelids fluttering. "Have ye killed the ones that shot me yet?"

Standing at the bedside, York shook his head. "No. I've had this blizzard to contend with. I fear those that done this to you are at large and likely gone from these parts."

Tulley frowned, more sad than anything else. "Tain't like you, Caleb York. Ye don't seem like the sort of lawman what would allow his faithful deputy to be shot down in the street like a dog."

York returned to his chair. "That's true, Tulley. But I do know who did this, at least I think I do."

Now Tulley sat up.

The sheriff rose and stuffed and fluffed the pillows behind his deputy, then again resumed his seat.

Tulley was saying, "*Who* done this then? Iffen ye must pursue the blackguard, I am here to tell ye that Jonathan P. Tulley be fit as a fiddle, and ready to ride!"

York shook a forefinger. "There will be no riding till this blizzard lets up, and the sun leans into all this drifted snow. As for who done it, have you heard of Luke Burnham?"

The deputy's eyes popped. " 'Burn 'Em' Burnham? 'deed I have. We have a poster on him. Quantrill rabble, I recall."

"That's right. And he has a bad grudge on me. I sent him to the graybar. You caught the brunt."

York filled his deputy in.

"Ye say," Tulley said, eyes narrowed, "he don't ride alone?"

"That poster of yours says he's leader of the Burnham gang. That's not alone. And Rita Filley saw him in town, day before you were bushwacked, with three no-accounts."

"Then ye must wait for me to get out of this here bed and on the back of Gertie."

Tulley's mule.

"I will welcome your support," York told him, "when the times comes. In fact, I brought you your scattergun." He gestured to where he'd leaned the weapon against the wall. "Might come in handy if looting breaks out."

This was nonsense, but York wanted Tulley to feel a part of things. Wanted the old desert rat to know that the sheriff considered him his valued deputy, even if bedridden.

"Never can tell," Tulley said, shutting an eye and leaving it that way a few seconds. "There's always them what takes advantage of the misfortune of others."

"Truer words." York rose. "I was out to

162

the Cullen ranch. They're hit hard by this. But Miss Cullen asked of you."

"Kind of her. She's a fine lady."

"She is indeed. Sends you her best."

"So kind, she be."

By the time York had reached the door, and looked back to bid his deputy good-bye, the old fellow was asleep again. Not snoring yet, but judging by Tulley's elaborate lip action, that would come soon enough.

When he entered the surgery's office, York found Doc Miller just coming in. The little pear-shaped physician looked beaten down as he brushed snow from his overcoat, then hung it and his hat on the coat tree. He removed his fogged-over glasses and tossed them on his desk.

"How's my patient?" Miller asked.

"I was going to ask you. But my diagnosis is, he's full of prunes."

Miller found a smile. "Nicely on the mend, yes."

The doctor gestured for York to follow him, and in moments they were in the medic's small kitchen, where Miller prescribed them both cups of coffee from the pot on his stove.

"He needs more rest, of course," Miller said, after a sip of the Arbuckles'. "But he's doing well. I wish I could say the same for the bulk of my patients."

York frowned. "How bad?"

The doctor sighed long and deep, shaking his head. He said, "These folks aren't used to this kind of cold. This preponderance of snow and ice. They try to keep the boardwalks outside their businesses cleared off when they don't have any customers, 'cept for the Mercantile, whose shelves are mostly bare now anyway. These fools should have just stayed inside, next to a damn stove or fireplace! I have enough cases of frostbite to make the '73 outbreak of cholera look like last year's chicken pox!"

York sipped coffee. "What can you do for it?"

The doctor rolled his eyes, shook his head. "Their idea of a remedy is worse than the ailment! Who told these fools to rub their frostbit feet in *snow*!"

"I've heard that myself."

"Well, it's nonsense. Dangerous nonsense." Miller wagged a finger at the sheriff. "Come the thaw, you're going to see a lot of strange-lookin' people walkin' around this town with fingers, toes, and ears and noses missin'. Warmth and light massage are all that can be done, really."

"What do you hear about Irish potatoes?"

"That they're good boiled — why?"

York finished his coffee. "Nothing." He got up. "I'm going down to the Victory and see how Miss Filley is faring."

The doc smiled and chuckled. Was that a twinkle in the old boy's eyes? "You're sweet on that *particular* filly, aren't you, Caleb?"

"Well, uh . . . she's a nice woman."

"Very nice. Very nice indeed. Were I younger, and not so devoted to my late wife's memory, you might have some competition there!"

"You know, Doc," York said, snugging his hat on, not bothering with the muffler now, "I might not mind."

The doc clearly didn't follow that, but York had no intention of explaining himself.

In the Victory, York was greeted by the warmth of the potbelly heating stove near the wall toward the front of the rear dance-floor area. The welcome heat, amplified by a cooking stove in the small kitchen behind the bar, was such that the sheriff climbed out of the frock coat and hung it and his hat on the pegs inside the front doors.

The tables in front were empty and the casino aspect of the facility shut down; and no one stood at the bar itself, its brass foot rail and spittoons ignored.

But the place was anything but empty.

Cowboys, their hats pushed back on their heads, sat in chairs commandeered from here and there in a semicircle three rows deep around the glowing potbelly. A few grouped in trios and quartets, facing each other to play cards, using empty chairs as tables, playing for small stakes. York noticed the telltale bedrolls piled against the wall on the other side of the room.

"We're the desert island," a familiar high-pitched yet throaty purr whispered, "where these sailors washed up in the storm."

A small, gentle hand had already settled on his arm as York turned to smile at the owner and hostess of the Victory Saloon. But though Rita Filley was very much her lovely self, she was not attired in one of her standard low-cut satin gowns that so emphasized the full bosom of her otherwise slender though shapely frame. Instead she was covered, chin to ankle, by a gray cotton blouse with a pink cameo pin, stand-up collar, and puffy sleeves with fitted cuffs, and a walking skirt of black twill.

And she wore no face paint whatever.

Was it possible she was even prettier without it?

She walked him to the bar, where head bartender Hub Wainwright — a big man with skimpy brown hair and broad shoul-

166

ders that indicated his secondary role as bouncer — was working alone.

"I'm afraid," York said, smiling at the fetching-looking woman, who appeared surprisingly like a prairie housewife at the moment, "a cold beer does not sound tempting today."

"We're way ahead of you," Rita said, then nodded to Hub, who disappeared into the kitchen. "Right now our own version of a hot toddy is the specialty of the house."

Soon a coffee cup was before him, and York again smiled at Rita and had a sip of the hot whiskey, honey, herbs, and spices. Then he had several more sips, before saying, "Just the ticket. So these boys were stranded here when the storm hit?"

"Or just decided from the start to ride it out in town," she said. "The hotel is full, so we're accommodating anyone who doesn't mind sleeping on the floor. And these cowhands all have bedrolls."

"Feeding them, too?"

Rita nodded, taking his arm again and walking him toward a table, where they sat in the warm path of the kitchen in back of the bar. York glimpsed the attractive colored girl who was Rita's new cook.

"By rescuing Mahalia from Hell Junction," Rita said, referring to a recent inci-

167

dent, "you did me a big favor. The girl works magic over a stove."

The high-yellow gal in black-and-white livery noticed him looking her way and smiled shyly and waved like a little girl. But she was full-growed, all right, and York returned the smile but quickly looked away. The last thing he needed right now was another good-looking woman in his life.

"I had plenty of provisions already laid in," Rita was saying with a shrug, "for our free lunches and suppers."

The saloon typically served up cold cuts, yellow cheese, rye bread, celery stalks, pretzels, peanuts, smoked herring, and dill pickles — salty fare to encourage thirsts that needed quenching.

"I take it you're not charging for lodging," York said, lifting the steaming coffee cup, "but that you *are* charging for hot toddies."

"Most perceptive," she said with a smile. "Only the sheriff drinks free. How is Deputy Tulley faring?"

"Doc says he should be fine," York said, "but the men who did it are well away by now."

"Are they?"

He frowned, leaning closer. "What do you mean by that, Rita?"

She sighed, then leaned in some herself, keeping her voice down. "I can't help but think about those three gunfighter-type characters who were so suddenly friendly with our local saddle shop man."

"I was there that night. Saw them myself, remember? Didn't recognize them. And I just went through the wanted circulars at the jailhouse. Of course, the son of a bitch who I figure shot Tulley, looking to kill me, *does* ride with three or four others."

"What son of a bitch?" The words sounded funny coming from Rita in her conservative attire.

"Luke Burnham."

Her eyes narrowed. "The man in the wanted circular you showed me."

York nodded. "He could very well be the man in the Confederate jacket you saw, with the mismatched eyes."

"Is he a famous outlaw?" She was relatively new to the West.

"Middling," York said. "But he's as dangerous as John Wesley Hardin, and he's a mite unhappy with me."

"Why unhappy?"

"I put him in prison for ten years."

"That would do it."

"But as for those that ride with him? I have no photographs, drawings, or descriptions as part of those circulars. And I checked for individual posters of anybody resembling those three we saw playing halfhearted poker with Bliss Maxwell. Nothing."

She said skeptically, "You figure they beat it out of Trinidad before the storm really got nasty."

"I do."

"And likely headed to Mexico, and figure when this squall blows over, you'll head that way yourself."

He sipped hot toddy and smiled. "Little time off can do wonders for a man."

"What if they're still here?"

"What if who's still here?" he asked innocently, but he knew what she meant.

"Those three 'friends' of Maxwell and the odd-eyed gent in the Rebel jacket." She leaned on an elbow, cocked her head. "Caleb, just yesterday . . . when this pretty white stuff started looking ugly to the locals, and the Mercantile had a run on supplies?"

"Yeah?"

"Well, I had one local canny enough to stop by and pick up some supplies right here at the Victory. Guess who that local was?"

"Bliss Maxwell."

"I heard you were a detective!" Rita's

sarcastic smile was a sideways thing. "And you know what supplies he bought? Three fancy bottles of rye from my private stock. Three-dollars-a-bottle whiskey."

York frowned. "I thought a bottle of whiskey at this establishment cost twenty-five cents."

"It does, but I told Maxwell I didn't care to sell any of my barroom supply, because I needed it myself. But said he could have the expensive stuff. The Denver stock, like you'd find in a top hotel."

York was frowning. "You know Bliss Maxwell to be much of a drinker?"

"I do not. I would say he's a one or two drink-a-night man. Of course, warming your stomach in this weather is an understandable pursuit."

He shook his head. "Not on three-buck-a-bottle whiskey it isn't. He buy any other provisions?"

She nodded. "Slabs of bacon. Corned beef. Smoked sausage." Archly she added, "You'd almost think he had guests."

York was ahead of her; but still — it just didn't make sense. "Why stick around Trinidad, before we really got snowed in?"

She shrugged one shoulder. "Well, didn't your friend Burnham mean to kill *you,* not Tulley? Maybe he realized he'd missed, and stuck around for a second try. Then got himself caught in this storm."

He thought about that, then admitted, "Maybe. Maybe."

She grasped his hands with hers and something earnest, and frightened, filled her face. "Why don't you stay here with me, Caleb. Avoid the office. Don't go to your room at the hotel. Don't bother prowling these streets — everybody's inside. Stay here on this desert island with me and the rest of the stranded souls. None of the others would have the . . . amenities . . . of your accommodations."

Before last night, he might have accepted. Likely would have. It wasn't as if he hadn't visited Rita's fancy quarters upstairs before. To him it seemed the scrape he was in with the two women in his life was damn near as dangerous as what he faced from Luke Burnham.

He drew his hands away from hers, then touched her face and smiled; she looked awfully troubled. Afraid for him, clearly. He liked that she, too, had both a hard and soft side. He finished the hot toddy. Rose.

"I have a paycheck to earn," he said.

He was getting into the frock coat when she was at his side. "If you get yourself killed, you lummox, I'll never speak to you again."

"Sounds fair." He put his hat on, not bothering with knotting it on with a muffler, then kissed her on the forehead and went out into the frigid whiteness that was Trinidad's Main Street.

Some of the boardwalk was cleared of drifting, parts weren't, but he was able to make his way to the livery stable in only twice the five minutes it would usually have taken.

The owner, burly blacksmith Lem Hansen, his hair a dirty yellow, his face a red-cheeked oval, was dressed no differently than any day — long-sleeve flannel shirt, canvas trousers with a leather apron, and a hat so misshapen its original form was unfathomable.

Though the blacksmith's clothing was plenty warm normally, today it would have left him frozen in minutes; but he had a heating stove going, and every stall had a horse in it, and the area outside the stalls was crowded with horses as well. Any horse in town whose owner didn't have access to a barn was paying to keep it here.

The blizzard was a boon to the livery.

York got the Burnham circular from his pocket and unfolded it and held it up for the blacksmith to consider. "Ever see this man? That scarred eye is an ungodly milky thing to behold. You wouldn't forget it."

Hansen didn't have to study the poster. "Yeah, I seen him. Confederate jacket, worn to hell. Three others with 'em. A skinny one what coughed. Two others who looked meaner than a foam-mouth dog."

"That's them."

"They kept their horses with me a while. They kept themselves with me, too. Slept in the stalls with their animals."

"When was this?"

Lem thought about it. "Not yesterday. The two days before that, it was. Nights, I mean. They lit out night 'fore last and I gathered they was about to start a considerable ride. It were already snowin'. Not as bad as it got. But *snowin'*."

So the night before last the Burnham gang had ridden out. What had their destination been? Mexico, chased by the threat of a storm? Las Vegas, maybe? To what purpose?

York asked, "You see which way they were headed?"

The blacksmith nodded, and pointed to the road that Main Street curved into past the livery, yawning north, where the horizon was home to the Sangre de Cristo Mountains.

Likely Las Vegas then. But that was a hell of a ride in these conditions.

"Thank you, Lem," York said.

He paused to stroke the dappled gelding and say a few soothing words to the animal, which had done so well for him, and not just in this instance.

"Always a pleasure to serve the law, Sheriff," Lem said with no enthusiasm and a nod. "Be they a reward?"

"Yes," York said. "And I intend to collect it."

The sheriff had already promised Cesar at the cantina a share and wasn't inclined toward further generosity.

The sheriff's next stop was the telegraph office, or it would have been, had he found the place open. Instead he faced a locked door with a message posted on its glass: "LINES DOWN."

So if the Burnham gang had gone to Las Vegas to take down the bank, say, or to some other town to do the same . . . or to rob some prosperous business or saloon, somewhere within riding distance . . . there was no way of knowing it, with the telegraph lines down.

He pressed on to the First Bank of Trinidad, where all was quiet. No lamps on, doors locked, no sign of life. Closed for business in the blizzard, no bothering with a posted message to that effect. Some things were just understood.

If Rita was right, Bliss Maxwell — apparently an honest local merchant — was playing host to four dangerous outlaws, holed up to wait out the storm and then, possibly, pick up where they left off . . .

. . . and shoot the sheriff instead of his deputy, this time.

York found that somewhat improbable, but another possibility tickled at his brain. What if Maxwell, in another, less honest life, had known Burnham? Perhaps ridden with him either in Quantrill's raiders or Burnham's first postwar gang, waylaying stagecoaches. In such a circumstance, the saddle shop man might have been coerced, essentially blackmailed, into providing a hideout for the current gang. A place to hole up if, for example, they had ridden to Las Vegas to raid the bank or some other substantial target.

It was guesswork, but rang true to him.

Intending to first check out Maxwell's living quarters above the saddle shop, York made a discovery out in back of the small barnlike structure that served as a workshop attached to the main building. Seemingly abandoned back there was a buckboard, its wagon box empty but for snow that had filled it up, its yoke unhitched and anchoring it.

York looked the wagon over, and saw words carved in, under the front between seat and toe board, saying JAMESON RANCH. That was one of the small ranches near town. What was its wagon doing here?

Then he noticed something else, not far from the buckboard. This was a part of Main that had nothing in back of it but vacant lots and scrubby desert stretching beyond, at least when it wasn't covered in white. A pile of snow, without the natural look of a drift or bank, had something leading to it.

Tiny spots of red.

He knelt over the spots, little droplets of scarlet spreading and soaking the snow, and suspected at once that violence had been done here. He was right to suspect this, but could not know that these spots had been left by a lunger in a coughing fit.

Nonetheless, the small red splotches, so stark against the white, seemed to lead to that pile of snow, which York used his gloved hands to paw away. This didn't take long before some actual violence was revealed, or at least the aftermath of same.

A man in a nice black suit — no overcoat

— lay on his back, as still as if he'd been frozen there. But that wasn't the case.

Bliss Maxwell — staring at the sky with snowflakes flocking his eyes, his mouth open as if words wanted out — had spilled far less blood than the crimson dots that had led York to him, surprisingly.

Surprisingly because Maxwell's throat had been cut.

Ear to ear.

CHAPTER EIGHT

Twenty minutes before his dead body was discovered by Sheriff Caleb York, Bliss Maxwell was playing gracious host to his four guests.

Luke Burnham and his boys — Jake Warlow, Moody Fender, and Ned Sivley — were seated at the kitchen table in Maxwell's well-furnished quarters above the saddle shop. They were eating the fare Maxwell had prepared for them — flapjacks and bacon and, again, whiskey-laced coffee.

Maxwell didn't join them in the fare. He'd had a bad night, entirely sleepless, and if his guests had been at all observant they would have noticed their host's red eyes and dark circles.

This scheme Luke Burnham had outlined the evening before, and pulled him into, had denied Maxwell of slumber. After thinking it through, turning it over and over in his mind, he finally came to a decision — he

179

must find a way to hit the brake on this runaway wagon.

But former general store proprietor Bliss Maxwell was, if anything, a salesman. And today he would have to make the sale of his lifetime.

The room was heavy with the aroma of melting fat, as more bacon sizzled and fried. He tended it and said, "Gentlemen, I beg you to reconsider. What you propose to do today is ill-advised. It's not the presence of Caleb York in this town that prompts me to say this, although that presents a danger in and of itself. No, it's the position you have put me in."

Burnham bit the end off a piece of crisp bacon, and chewed as he said, "What position is that, Silas?"

Maxwell had given up on getting his old comrade to stop calling him by his real first name.

The merchant swiveled from the stove to them. "Luke, if you take down this bank, the *Trinidad* bank, it will undoubtedly come back on me. We were *seen* together — Jake, Moody, Ned, and me — at the Victory."

Calling the gang members by their first names was an attempt to make him seem more an ally.

"And," Maxwell continued, "the *four* of

us were at the cantina together." His chin
came up. "I didn't mention this before, but
York came around here, the day after his
deputy was shot, sniffing around."

"No," Burnham said with a frown, pouring rye into his coffee. "You *didn't* mention
that."

"Which makes it a certainty," Maxwell
said, pressing on, "in the wake of a bank
robbery, that the sheriff will make a return
visit to check up on me. He may well
suspect that I'm billeting you."

"Silas, old friend," Burnham said, after a
sip of coffee and rye, "hasn't it got through
to you yet that I would like nothing *better*
than to have Caleb York knock on that
door?"

Maxwell came over and stood next to the
seated outlaw leader. "York is no fool. If he
thinks there's the slightest chance four
desperados, one of whom is out to get him,
are holed up here? He won't come alone.
He'll come the way you entered Lawrence,
Kansas — *in force*. After raising a posse.
Might even burn us out — he's as ruthless
as you, Luke, in his way."

Fender, frowning as he cut a syrup-
drenched flapjack with a fork, said to the
outlaw leader, "Your old buddy Silas is an
excitable type, Luke. Tell him I won't put

up with havin' my digestion trifled with."

But Warlow said, "Luke, he's right about York, and you damn well know it. What say we *don't* burrow in here till the snow stops and melts some. It's not comin' down as hard now. We could hit that bank and ride out *today*. There's two horses down in that little barn, and sure as hell plenty of saddles. We can grab a couple more rides from the livery on our way out."

"You grow yourself a short memory, Jake?" Burnham asked. "You don't recall our several jaunts in this winter weather, last few days? *No*. We stay here. We'll be ready for anything York might bring."

A small mutiny seemed to be brewing, though, as Sivley said, "I think we're invitin' ruin if we dig in here, after hearin' what Maxwell says. I say we hit the bank and vamoose. You can come back after you spend some time down in sunny May-hee-co, when Caleb York has forgot all about you and us."

The others agreed, and for several minutes the three men made it clear to their boss they weren't staying.

Back tending his bacon at the stove, Maxwell let this go on a while, then said, "Fellas . . . you don't even know if that bank has enough money in it *worth* stealing."

Burnham, scowling, said, "Banks *always* got money, and money's *always* worth stealing."

"I'm going to respectfully hold you," Maxwell said, turning to them again, "to the original plan. To what we originally agreed upon. You have twenty thousand dollars. I am willing to forgo my cut and yet share my lodgings with you until the blizzard subsides and you feel it's safe to move on."

"Do you," Burnham said flatly.

"I do. I have laid in generous provisions for your stay. That whiskey you're pouring into your Arbuckles' cost me three dollars a bottle, and all of that, and the roof over your head and the warm beds to sleep in, are yours. No charge. No cut."

Fender, frowning so hard it made him look even more stupid, said, "Why the hell would you do that?"

Maxwell came over and leaned in, putting his hands on the table. "Because if you are caught, gents, I will be swept up in it. And if you get away, after hitting the Trinidad bank, my having been seen with you could easily land me in jail as an accomplice to a crime spree that your boss man here informs me has *already* included four murders."

183

Burnham growled, "You weren't in on them."

"I'm part of all this, Luke. I could hang for those killings, even if you never do. And even if no charges are brought against me, the suspicion would remain. I'd be finished in Trinidad. The business I've invested my life savings in, and worked so hard to build here, would be tainted. Eventually driven out of existence. *That* is why I would do that."

Maxwell lurched away from the table and went over to look out the window over the sink. He stared out at endless white. Trembling. With anger. With fear.

Quietly he said, "You'll haul that banker over there to unlock that safe and it'll make a witness of him, if you leave him behind, or you'll kill him to avoid it . . . and either way you make something horrible out of my future."

Behind him, Luke Burnham raised a calming hand to his boys, who were all frowning, with Fender halfway out of his chair till his boss gestured him back down.

The outlaw leader rose and walked over to the slump-shouldered Maxwell, whose hands were against the sink, bracing himself, as if he might otherwise collapse.

"You talk sense, Silas," Burnham said.

184

"We'll do it your way."

Maxwell let out air, looking up, and his expression in the glass of the window showed his relief. And then the glass revealed the quick movement of Burnham gripping the merchant's hair in his left hand while the right hand swung around with something steel and gleaming.

The last coherent thought Maxwell had on this earth was that the steel, gleaming thing was a Bowie knife.

The cut throat initially sent blood splashing against the window glass, then Burnham held the head of the dying man over the sink to let more blood spill over the drain. At the table, Fender was grinning while Sivley and Warlow absently worked on their breakfasts.

Burnham dragged the corpse away from the sink; no blood was flowing now — dead men, Burnham knew from long experience, did not bleed. He dropped the late merchant to the floor, where the body landed like a sack of grain that had been poorly aimed at the back of a wagon.

"Ned," Burnham said, nodding to the pump attached to the sink, "wash that out. Moody, get something to clean off that window glass."

Fender, of course, was irritated. "Jesus,

Luke! Why didn't you just plug him? I didn't hire on for no damn house-cleaning chores."

"Maybe you never noticed," Burnham said, "but guns make noise. Even in a blizzard, folks react to a gunshot. Whereas a blade may be messy, but it sure don't call attention to itself."

Fender and Sivley looked at each other, the latter shrugged, then so did the former, and they got to work with those chores.

Then Burnham went over and got himself more bacon and coffee, skipping the rye this time. He sat and sipped and chewed and thought.

When the sink and windows had been cleaned up, Sivley and Fender — bloody towels in hand — turned and looked at their boss.

Burnham pointed a forefinger at Warlow. "Take our dead friend down and bury him in the snow out back. You and Moody do the hauling. Sivley, you go on ahead of 'em and have a good look-see and make sure nobody's about. Can't be having gawkers."

"So," Warlow said, getting up slowly, frowning in slightly confused thought, "does this change anything?"

Burnham turned his eyes on them, both the good and the milky one. Gestured with

186

open hands.

"We'll come back here and enjoy the hospitality of our dead host," he said. "Whiskey and food and warm beds, like the man said. In a day or two, this storm will let up and we'll be on our way."

"What about Caleb York?"

Burnham made a face, then shrugged. "If he turns up, I'll deal with him. If he doesn't . . . our dearly departed former associate on the floor over there may have been right. I'll have to let my little grudge go for now, and be satisfied with the hauls from two banks. I can return on my own time, when the weather's friendlier, and I've slipped York's mind."

Sivley coughed into his bloody towel, adding to it, then said, "If we're fixin' to hole up here, after all, when darkness comes? We should haul Maxwell's remains out some, a ways off from the town. Can't have somebody stumblin' over him."

"Can't have that," Burnham agreed. "But for now — get that bastard out of here. Can't you fools see I'm tryin' to eat my breakfast?"

Half an hour later, Caleb York was prowling the living quarters of the late Bliss Maxwell, his .44 in hand, his black frock coat sweeping like a cape behind him. The guests of the dead man he'd discovered in the snow out back were nowhere to be seen.

But the signs of them were everywhere. York had come in through the kitchen, shouldering open the door and ready to go into blazing battle. What he found, in a chamber redolent of bacon grease, was a table with dirty dishes on it, and a sink where on the counter nearby a few telltale drops of blood had been missed by the cleanup crew.

Those few droplets seemed to confirm his notion that Maxwell had been killed up here, as the corpse down below was accompanied by no bleeding out, meaning the man was dead already when he was given his temporary wintery grave. The sheriff — not knowing the blood spots near the mound of snow came from Ned Sivley coughing them up — was surprised there had been any blood at all.

And stuffed in a drawer were two very blood-soaked towels, starting to get crusty but mostly still wet.

Elsewhere in the apartment somebody hadn't flushed the fancy indoor privy and York thoughtfully did it for him. There was a claw-foot bathtub that nobody seemed to have used lately. Facing bedrooms in the hallway had the rumpled sheets and blankets of careless guests, but what interested York most were the saddlebags.

A pair, slung over a chair, in either room. Their pouches contained sacks of paper money and coin — some of the paper money banded in Bank of Las Vegas wrappers. York made a quick tally that took the jackpot into the thousands — fifteen at least.

Before, there could have been little doubt in his mind that Burnham and his bunch were the men who'd holed up here, including slitting their host's throat. Now there was no doubt at all. The gang had ridden through the night to Las Vegas, knocked over the bank, and ridden back to hide out in Maxwell's digs, and wait out the weather.

York was able to transfer all of the money into the two pouches of one saddlebag. He could take it with him and walk it down to the jailhouse and put the stolen money in his safe. Still, this was the west end of Main, near the church, and his office was at the east end, near the livery stable. Not a terribly long walk, even in this storm.

But the men who took this money, and who had been staying here, were still in town. Where? Up to what?

Perhaps he should wait here for them to come back, to emerge from the cold into his warm welcome. . . .

That door he'd shouldered through, however, had splintered some and might give his presence away. Waiting outside didn't appeal to him — wherever he positioned himself, he could be come up on from behind. And it was still damn cold, for just standing around.

Were they on foot? He didn't figure they were on horseback, otherwise they'd have taken along the saddlebags of loot.

What the hell were they up to in Trinidad?

Maybe this was personal. Maybe this was about finding and killing a certain Caleb York before the Burnham boys continued south to a warmer clime and no extradition. That would put them out there somewhere in his town, looking for him — maybe setting up an ambush at his office, possibly taking over one of the adobe homes in the barrio across the way.

They would certainly not go up to the Victory, where Rita would recognize them. And little else in town was open for business. Seemed unlikely they'd try to take down a second bank in two days; the establishment was among those closed, and York didn't figure any of the Burnham gang knew how to crack or blow a safe. The wanted circular made no mention of such rarefied skills.

Damn!
What were they up to?

Peter Godfrey was a man of modest size but considerable dignity.

At thirty-seven he was already properly white haired including his eyebrows and his well-trimmed mustache, full of face, and with a slight potbelly to indicate he could afford to eat well, and with a voice deeper and richer than one might expect from someone who stood five foot five inches.

His wardrobe was deep and rich, too, from silk to tweed, and filled a closet in the apartment that took up the third floor of the bank building. His sartorial selections ran to frock coats in black, gray, and other dark colors; brocade and embroidered waistcoats; half a dozen sets of collars and cuffs; trousers, predominantly black but with a few light color and patterned variations mixed in; a variety of ties, bow, four-in-hand, and English square; and several jaunty Homburg hats.

Godfrey, a shopkeeper's son, was quite aware that an appearance of personal prosperity carried as much weight in banking as a reputation for reliability and having a good head for business. His quietly friendly, restrained manner had served him well as a teller at the Provincial Bank of Santa Fe, and led to his eventual appointment as vice president in charge of loans.

Raymond L. Parker of Denver, one of the owners of the Santa Fe bank, had selected Godfrey much as a stage director might cast a play, to take over the leading role at the First Bank of Trinidad — a small operation now, but one that would grow. A spur was coming in that would make a railhead out of a little town already surrounded by rich cattle land.

As for Parker, he'd once been a partner in the Cullen ranch, the Bar-O, and continued to have business interests in the little community. On offering the top position to Godfrey, Parker had explained that this great opportunity had its risks — First Bank had suffered setbacks, including a robbery last year that had involved the previous president . . . who in fact had lived in these very quarters above the bank (with Dr. Miller on the floor between).

And those living quarters had their own troubled history.

Not that there was anything to complain about where the accommodations were concerned. The living room boasted Victorian-style furnishings that had no doubt cost a pretty penny, including buttonback sofa, wingback chairs, marble-top tables, and Oriental carpet. The bedroom was similarly well furnished, the heavy dark wood against gold-and-brown striped wallpaper. A guest room and study filled out the posh surroundings.

In that study, at a rolltop desk, the previous bank president had either committed suicide or been murdered, depending on which scuttlebutt you believed.

Godfrey found little reason to go into the room.

Not that he was squeamish or believed in ghosts or any such nonsense. Nor did he think it likely that he would ever encounter violence in his respectable line of work. Bank robberies were rare as hen's teeth. And hen's teeth *were* rare . . . weren't they?

Right now he was in the kitchen. He was fully dressed, in frock coat, waistcoat, and trousers, even his well-polished black Oxfords, as if he were prepared for a normal workday or perhaps ready to go to church on a Sunday. Of course this was not Sunday, nor was it a normal workday — but the clothing was warm, and the cold that gripped little Trinidad, which shivered under a white blanket not at all warming, was like nothing Peter Godfrey — who'd grown up in the Southwest — had ever experienced.

Also, the cooking stove in the kitchen was a wonderful source of warmth. He normally dined at the hotel restaurant, and knew little of cooking — he was a married man and his wife Faith was wonderful in the kitchen. But he did know how to make a decent pot of coffee, and had a cup before him now. Faith would be proud.

The wind sang discordantly and occasionally howled, as if objecting to its own inability to maintain pitch. Godfrey couldn't sing any better than this Norther, despite his sonorous speaking voice. He'd just mouth the words of hymns in church.

Faith had a wonderful voice, as pretty as her sweet face. So did his little girl, Grace, ten. His boy, Andrew, eight, had unfortunately inherited his father's lack of talent in that area.

How he missed them.

In the fall, with any luck, they would be here with him in Trinidad in the house that Parker was having built for him, as a perquisite of the bank president position. For now, however, Faith and the children remained in Santa Fe. She was firm about letting Andrew and Grace, who liked their teachers and their friends, finish out the school year. And the timing would be propitious for the new house.

Faith pledged to visit in the summer.

So for now it was a lonely life, a bachelor's life, but without the comfort of female company. He was a faithful husband, not tempted by the saloon girls, some of whom were quite fetching, and willing to rent their charms. Well, perhaps he was tempted — but not likely to give in. His position in the community, the reputation he was still building here, would not allow that.

But he missed them so, his little family.

He would have been ashamed if anyone had seen him, a well-dressed man sitting there in the kitchen, quietly crying into a handkerchief over the absence of the family he so dearly missed. He would have felt a fool, and might have been viewed as such by many.

Some, though, might have been wise enough to see that this was a good man, whose qualities went well beyond tailored apparel.

Someone knocked on the door.

On the exterior stairway alongside the bank building, four men in dusters were staggered up the top three steps and the landing.

Luke Burnham knew damn well that

milky eye of his took some folks aback. So he'd positioned Jake Warlow outside the bank president's apartment — after all, the handsome bastard had charm and the gift of gab. Meanwhile Burnham took the top step, Fender the next down, and Sivley the last — you never knew when that lunger might start coughing.

Warlow's knock was answered and the door opened, more than a crack, less than all the way — enough that Burnham, tucked against the brick wall, could see a reflection of the man within on the door glass.

"Yes?" said the distinguished-looking, white-haired gent — a little feller with a potbelly, dressed up to beat the band. What for?

"Mr. Godfrey?"

"Yes?"

"Name's Jacob Jones." Warlow pointed vaguely toward the street. "I work for Miss Filley at the Victory. Maybe you seen me there — behind the bar?"

"No, I, uh . . . I've been there occasionally, but I don't recall seeing you, sir."

Warlow grinned. "Well, I woulda been wearin' a shirt and tie and apron with my hair slicked back. Might look a mite different, off-duty. Anyhow, somebody ran in and told Miss Filley there's a disturbance over here at your bank. She asked that we come inform you of such."

The banker's alarm was almost comical. "A disturbance? What sort of disturbance? Did you see anything going on down there?"

Warlow hugged himself and shivered. "Might I step inside, Mr. Godfrey? Seems we're both gettin' colder than need be. You'd think this snow would wear itself out, wouldn't you?"

The door opened and Godfrey gestured for Warlow to enter, which he did. Burnham, Fender, and Sivley followed quick, surprising their host, who hadn't seen the trio on the steps below the landing. The door slammed shut behind them.

"Who are these people?" the banker asked Warlow, mildly indignant, then looking from face to face. "What's the meaning of this?"

Warlow smiled, closing the door on the cold. "Miss Filley thought you might need some help, Mr. Godfrey. What with that disturbance at your bank?"

The banker nodded at the men, smiling uncertainly. "Well, I appreciate that. What exactly sort of disturbance is it? Did you notice something going on in there, before you came up? Have you sought out the sheriff?"

Warlow said, "He doesn't seem to be

around. And it does seem quiet down there now."

"What sort of disturbance in the bank are we *talking* about? Be *clear,* man!"

Burnham stepped up and withdrew his hand from a slit in the duster — a hand gripping the Colt Lightning revolver — and tweaked the tip of the banker's nose with the nose of the gun.

"Someone's about to rob it," he said.

Caleb York needed to make sure the noise he'd made bursting into Bliss Maxwell's apartment hadn't alerted the Burnham gang and sent them scurrying into hiding, right there on the premises, somewhere. He slung the saddlebag of loot over his shoulder — it was awkward but he wanted to keep his hands on it — and looked into the matter.

A door off the hallway, just before you got to the indoor privy, opened onto a stairwell down to the saddle shop. As York descended slowly, the familiar musky oiled leather odor rose from a shop that lay in darkness, its window given scant light by a day blotted out by white. He had a little box of safety matches in his coat pocket, and with his .44 in his right hand, York held the wooden match in his left and his thumbnail flicked it to light. The sudden flare of it illuminated a room empty of anything but the saddle shop's wares, then the match settled itself into a smaller guiding light.

But he carefully prowled the shop, making sure no one knelt behind a display case or in back of a saddle on its wooden stand. When he was convinced he was alone in this outer area, he went back behind the main display case, into a back room with more saddles on stands, and a cubbyhole at right — its door open — with a small bed and a dresser and mirror. Some Catholic images were on the wall.

These were clearly the Mexican saddle maker's sleeping quarters, with hardly enough room to accommodate its occupant, let alone provide a hiding place for any of the Burnham gang. And Maxwell's man Juan was not in sight.

Not in a pile of snow with his throat cut, too, York hoped.

Beyond was the workshop in the barnlike structure attached to the rear of the building. Again York thumbed a match and brandished the .44. Two horses were in the stalls, stirring at his presence, and the work area appeared to have been cleared, for what reason York didn't know.

Then it occurred to him that the dead horses he'd seen on the road might have belonged to the Burnham gang, and these two animals might have been stolen from the Jameson Ranch buckboard. Would be a good bet, he feared, that the original riders on the wagon were murder victims who would turn up when the snow melted. And this cleared area might have been meant to accommodate two horses that never arrived.

Satisfied that the saddle shop building was empty of outlaws, York returned to the shop itself, pulled over a saddle on its stand by the window and climbed on, as if he were about to ride somewhere.

But all he wanted was a good view on Main, or as good a one as the still falling snow allowed. It was mid-morning, but you'd never know it. He was angled right, to get a look down the street, where both the bank and the Victory were in view. The bank was dark, but lamps in upstairs windows over businesses burned yellow, and the Victory windows burned, as well, campfires in a cold wilderness.

Caleb York — on his stationary saddle, his .44 in hand, his black frock coat blending him with the darkened shop, saddlebag of recovered bank booty on the rear of the stand — waited and watched.

CHAPTER NINE

Peter Godfrey faced the menacing men in his kitchen, their dusters dripping melting snow on his floor. All four towered over him, their leader training a gun on Godfrey, who wondered if he would ever see his wife and children again. The banker wished he could excuse himself for just a moment, before this confrontation continued, to go to the bedroom where the framed photograph on his night table might allow him a few moments with Faith, Grace, and Andrew.

But such an interruption was an impossibility, of course, and as he looked at these men — their leader a fearsome creature with a milky eye and a face devoid of compassion, the one who'd knocked at his door a handsome fellow but on closer look a rough sort despite his smiling ways, another who seemed to sneer at the world, and a skinny one who periodically coughed into a bloody handkerchief. That last one was already on the road to death, but as things stood, would be still alive when Godfrey was gone.

He must handle these men. He handled depositors and customers seeking loans with friendly firmness; he would hide his fear and address them as fellow human beings, though he suspected they had lived lives that made them something less than that.

The leader was saying, "Is there a back way into that bank?"

"There is," Godfrey said. He found a small smile and gestured to the kitchen table. "Gentlemen, would you sit so that we might discuss this? I have coffee on the stove and you've been out in the cold. I assure you we can deal with this situation in a civilized manner."

The hideous-eyed one said, in a voice vaguely touched with the South, "There'll be no sittin', and no discussion. You will do as we say or pay the highest price."

Godfrey raised a hand in a gentle gesture. "I will do as you say, sir. I will follow your directions, gentlemen. I have no desire to place Mammon before my very life. But I have a proposition. Could you spare a few moments, before we head downstairs?"

The milky-eyed one scowled, but the handsome devil put a hand on his leader's arm and said, "He's cooperatin', boss. Let him talk. He seems to have somethin' to say."

The other two, though both frowning, said nothing.

The outlaw leader nodded, in a barely perceptible fashion, and said, "All right. Talk, banker."

He did: "Our cash on hand, right now, is in the neighborhood of ten thousand dollars."

"Hell of a cheapjack neighborhood," the leader said skeptically, "for a ranchin' hub like this."

Godfrey acknowledged that with a nod. "But this is a slow time of year, when the ranches have laid off many of their cowboys. Payroll needs are less, so fewer funds are kept on hand. Further, we make it a practice to regularly transfer bags of paper money and coin to Denver, to the Union Bank, another of the Parker firms. Wells Fargo made such a run just a week and a half ago."

The grin in the outlaw leader's face somehow made that odd eye worse to behold. "Here's how it's gonna work, Godfrey. You'll open that safe of yours and we'll take however much is in it."

The banker raised a palm, again gently. "I understand that is your intention. But let me make a counter-proposal. My personal deposit in First Bank is four thousand dollars. If you will settle for that, and leave the balance behind, I will not report the robbery. You would not be pursued, and please understand that a posse consisting of those whose money you have stolen — the depositors in this bank — would only be too eager to help Sheriff Caleb York track you down."

His duster-draped guests were thinking.

"I must also in fairness inform you, gentlemen," Godfrey said, "that this bank suffered a robbery last year that almost brought it down. While the money was largely recovered, the fact that my presidential predecessor was — as they say — 'in on' the robbery, well . . . rather dampened the local populace's faith in banking in general. If I could avoid what you intend to do by essentially paying you *not* to do it, I might well prevent the collapse of this institution."

The sour-faced outlaw said, "And you'd be out of a job."

"I would indeed."

But he would be alive.

The four men said nothing. They didn't even exchange glances. Each was lost in his own calculations.

Then the milky-eyed leader asked, "Where

is York now?"

"I frankly don't know. I doubt he's bothering with making rounds in this weather. The town is virtually frozen in place, everyone inside seeking warmth and shelter, all the shops closed." The banker shrugged. "I *do* know that yesterday the sheriff rode out to the Bar-O to see how they were faring."

The handsome outlaw muttered, "Bar-O's the biggest ranch around here."

"Yes," Godfrey said, "a twenty-minute ride on the road north, in normal circumstances. The sheriff is, uh, good friends with Willa Cullen — the Bar-O was her late father's ranch."

"By 'good friends,' " the handsome one said, his grin turning lascivious, "you mean York may have stayed the night?"

"The storm may have dictated that," Godfrey said ambiguously. "At any rate, if he's back in town, I'm not aware of it."

This was not a lie, but Godfrey hadn't been out of his quarters today, so really had no way to know. And he wanted very much to sell his proposal to these men. Their leader had said no discussion, and yet that was precisely what they'd been engaging in for several minutes now.

Godfrey said, "You would have to take my word that I would not report this incident, and that I would pledge not to identify any of you, when photographs and drawings are brought to my attention."

But Godfrey would be alive, and he felt confident that he could discreetly inform Raymond L. Parker of what had happened, and that Godfrey had handled it . . . and be reimbursed for his own life savings of four thousand dollars.

The bank president risked a smile. "What do you say, gentlemen? Do we have a deal?"

The skinny one with the cough, the sour-faced fellow, and the handsome devil were finally exchanging glances now, shrugging, eyebrows lifting, obviously seeing the banker's proposal as reasonable.

But the outlaw leader said, "No. We'll take it all, thanks. And you can identify us till Judgment Day. I do not give a damn."

"Well, I, uh . . . thought perhaps you might . . ."

The milky-eyed outlaw grabbed the banker by a coat lapel and jerked him up onto his toes, leaning into the smaller man's face, till they were all but nose to nose.

"Banker, I *want* you to describe me to Caleb York. I want him to know I came to his town and took his town's money. I would be good and goddamn *grateful* to you if you did!"

Would that be enough to keep Peter Godfrey alive? The banker could only wonder.

"Get your keys and put your overcoat on," the outlaw leader said to Godfrey. "And everybody plaster on a smile, including . . . 'specially . . . you, Mr. Bank President. If any town folk are out there takin' the air and freezin' their damn tails off, they should see four fellers happy as hell to be in each other's company."

Godfrey did as he was told.

But he now knew he would have to rely on something else he'd deposited in his bank, something whose existence the bank president had not shared with the outlaws — the Colt Model 1877 revolver called a Thunderer with its short two-and-a-half-inch barrel and its long .41 rounds, tucked in a little drawer under the bags of money in the safe.

In his hospital gown and under warm covers, Jonathan P. Tulley — alone in his sickroom in the apartment of Dr. Albert Miller, out dealing with the frostbite epidemic — stirred but did not awaken due to the heavy footsteps on the staircase along the side of the building.

But conversation on the floor above, and more movement, finally did bring him

around. He frowned, as male voices continued, one recognizable as that of the bank
president who lived up there. Fully awake
now, Tulley heard the call of nature as well,
and used the chamber pot before climbing
back under the sheets and blankets.

The talk went on, some of it — from a
rough voice he did not recognize — loud
and stirred up, which set Tulley to frowning. He could not make anything out, but
that was not the point. The deputy had been
in this bed for two days and not heard a
peep out of the upstairs resident, who
seemed to have had no visitors at all in that
time.

Nor had he noticed much noise seeping
up from the bank below, during its business
hours; but then he'd been pretty well out
on the laudanum the doc gived him, and
today the establishment was likely closed,
what with the snow and all.

Nonetheless, Tulley just burrowed into the
bed clothes, figuring a man had a right to
entertain and sometimes arguments broke
out between friends. What business was it
of his?

But then boots came clomping back down
those outside steps, a whole damn herd of
folk it seemed, and he sat up, annoyed, and
frowned toward the sound. He got out of

bed and padded over in his bare feet to his window to see who had disrupted his slumber, but nobody was out there at all. Main Street was still all drifted over and snow just kept coming down, maybe not so damn heavy now, but still a-comin'.

So he shrugged, went over, and climbed in bed, tucked himself in and was almost back to sleep when noise from below — nothing big, not a runaway train or nothin', just more talk and movement — got him to thinking.

That was the bank down there, under him. And if somebody was up to somethin' in that bank, when it was closed, that *would* be Deputy Tulley's business.

Yet he could tell one of those voices was the bank president's, softer than the other male voices he could make out, but that was Mr. Godfrey, all right.

Tulley climbed out of the bed and his bare feet took him to the scattergun leaning against the wall by the window. Just what he might do with the weapon, he couldn't have said. But it seemed like he ought to have that in hand, even though he hadn't figured out what, if anything, he should do.

Jake Warlow had ridden with Lucas Burnham long enough to be well-acquainted with the outlaw leader's ruthless ways. Not that Warlow was the squeamish type. And he was grateful to Burnham for the opportunities the man had provided — Jake would never have been able to pull in so damn many dollars these past several years if he'd restricted himself to earning honest ones.

But Warlow had a feeling the boss was going to kill this banker, once that safe got emptied, and somehow it just didn't seem right. The stuffy little Godfrey feller was following orders just fine, and that proposal the bank president had made, to pay them off with his own money, had seemed damn white of him. If Jake were leader of this outfit, he'd have grabbed that four grand and the promise of no robbery reported and no Caleb York posse to dog their trail.

Yet from the start of this thing, ol' "Burn 'Em" Burnham had been so tied up in knots over getting even with this York that it had screwed things up damn near as bad as the weather. Warlow didn't like that, didn't like that one little bitty bit. You keep your feelings out of it. They were professionals, weren't they? They should *act* like professionals!

Still, Burnham was the boss, and Warlow respected him, in addition to fearing that milky-eyed son of a bitch, who a while back he'd seen kill a fellow gang member that crossed him. Not *double*-crossed him, either — just somebody they rode with who wouldn't go along with what Burnham wanted.

So, like the banker, Warlow was just doing as he was told. He went down the steps first, followed by Sivley, then Godfrey, Fender, and finally Burnham. All four outlaws had their sidearms in hand under the dusters. Everybody kept a smile on their face — even Moody.

No one saw them, or at least it didn't appear anyone had. The biggest threat of being seen came from the building on the corner across the way, the Victory Saloon, one of the few establishments in Trinidad open for business in the blizzard, though its front doors were shut tight and no honky-tonk or casino sounds were bleeding out.

In knee-high snow, the five men trudged back behind the big brick building, flakes swirling around them. The alley behind the bank was hidden under a heavy blanket of white, on the other side of which were the backyards of dwellings. That the snow wasn't coming down as hard now was not enough to invite anyone out into this wintery world, which was more purgatory than wonderland. The closest thing to a witness was a snowman some child had built early on, itself buried in white up to its waist, its coal eyes looking hysterical.

All of the men, banker included, had to kick away at the snow in front of the rear door, to clear the way enough for Godfrey to work a key in the lock and open it.

Soon they were inside the big single room that was the bank, which sported the expected fine wood, brass fittings, and marble floor, with a trio of barred cashier windows in a long polished counter. Going in the back way put them on the teller side of those windows. A big rectangular iron safe rested against the back wall under a map of New Mexico Territory.

The bank president had no office, rather a big fancy desk behind a low wooden railing with a gate, over to the left as the men came in.

The outlaw leader's Colt Lightning was out from under the duster. Everyone in the gang had his gun in hand now. The big room, with no lamps lit, was fairly dark and it was doubtful anyone could see what was happening through the front windows. The counter with its teller cages blocked things as well. The only witness seemed to be the storm itself, which continued its moaning, howling, and whistling, as if Nature herself had set off an alarm, only to be ignored.

"Get to it," Burnham told the banker.

"Yes, sir," the captive said.

The safe was so big, and the banker so short, that Godfrey didn't have to bend down to work the dial on the big Mosler Company cast-iron safe, black with gold edging. The combination clicked in place and the little man swung open the big door.

Now Godfrey knelt. He fished around inside.

Burnham said, "What are you up to?"

"Nothing, sir." He turned and handed the leader a folded-over empty canvas bag, the size of a mail sack. "That's what we fill up with the smaller bags, in preparation for the Wells Fargo runs."

Warlow and Fender stood to one side as the banker passed out bags of cash and then coin to them to fill the bigger bag, which said FIRST BANK OF TRINIDAD in stenciled black. Burnham just supervised, keeping his Colt trained on the banker, who knelt at the open safe as if at an altar. Sivley was keeping a general lookout between coughs of red into an increasingly wretched handkerchief.

As the banker handed bags of money back to the thieves, Burnham asked him, "Is there any money in the cashier drawers?"

"No, sir. After closing each day, the tellers run a tally and everything goes in the safe."

The bigger bag of smaller bags was soon full, held together at the top by a wide wooden snap.

For a few moments, the bank president, kneeling there, stared into the safe.

Burnham stepped up behind him. "Is that it?"

Godfrey didn't answer.

"Is that *it,* I said!"

The banker gulped — it was quite audible — then he said quietly, "Yes. That's it."

The outlaws could not know that the banker had decided against removing the compact revolver from its little hiding place in a small drawer under the safe's main compartment.

"That's it, all right," Burnham said, and he placed the nose of his Colt against the nape of the neck of the kneeling man. He thumbed back the hammer and the cocking click was itself like a gunshot in the big empty room.

Warlow put his hand on Burnham's wrist and clamped down, jerking it away from its target.

"No," Warlow said.

"No?" Burnham bared his teeth. *"You're* in charge now, Jake?"

"I'm not in charge. But you said it before

214

— guns make noise. And as for what you used earlier . . ."

The Bowie knife.

". . . you leave this man butchered and we'll have every lawman in the Territory down on us. Caleb York will be the least of our worries."

Burnham glowered, but he was thinking.

Surprisingly, Moody said, "Godfrey here's done everything we asked. He's a friendly little guy. Leave him be."

Sivley laughed. "Hey, he's crying!"

And he was.

Warlow said, "Damnit, Luke — let him be. Hey! Banker!"

"Y-yes . . ."

"You still willin' to promise not to identify us if they start showin' you pitchers?"

"Y-yes . . ."

"You heard us call each other by name. You gonna remember those names?"

"N-no . . ."

" 'Cause iffen you do, we might just come back and finish the job."

Burnham said to the banker, "Where do your people hail from?"

That seemed to throw Godfrey, who was doing his best not to weep, but his best wasn't good enough. "What?"

"Where do you hail from?"

"Originally . . . Kentucky."

That was not true. Godfrey was from Iowa. But he had heard the tinge of Southern accent in the outlaw leader's voice.

"Find something," Burnham said, "to bind him."

One teller drawer had twine in it and they used that, tying the banker's hands behind him and his ankles together, and stuffing a hanky — not one of Sivley's! — in his mouth as a gag. They left the little man on the floor behind the counter, where he could not be seen through a window on the street.

Pointing toward the rear, out of the bank president's earshot, Burnham said, "We go out the way we came in. Ned and me will head back to Maxwell's. Jake, you and Moody go down to the livery and buy or take a couple of horses. Now let's go!"

Before they left, Warlow nodded to the bound banker, who nodded back, gratitude in his expression despite the hanky wadded in the man's mouth.

As the four outlaws came out from behind the building, Warlow was feeling good — they had picked up an easy ten grand to plump up the disappointing Las Vegas haul. And he was pleased at saving the banker's life. He didn't like to think of himself a bad

216

man, just someone who'd had some nasty breaks and took some wrong turns. Running with the likes of Luke Burnham, he reasoned, could make anybody think they'd gone bad.

Warlow paused in front of the bank, knee-deep in snow, and said to Fender, "We don't need saddles. There's plenty back at Maxwell's to choose from."

Fender nodded and offered up a rare smile, which disappeared when his face got splattered with blood and bits of gore when Warlow's head, handsome face and all, got blown off his neck by a double-barreled shotgun from above.

Not long before, Caleb York could not see — from his perch on a saddle on its stand near a window of Maxwell Boots, Harness, and Saddle Depot — the movement within the bank building. That was taking place too deep into the large single room that was the bank, where additionally no lamps were lit.

So he had no notion, no suspicion, that a robbery was taking place even as he kept watch. He was, in fact, fighting boredom, reminded of the many hours of vigil he'd maintained in his time as a Wells Fargo detective. He'd spent days and nights in high rocks watching through army signal glasses a farmhouse where outlaws might rendezvous. For seemingly countless hours he'd sat in hotel lobbies waiting for a suspect to show.

Not his favorite part of that job.

But his boredom vanished, and he sat up straight in his store-bound saddle, when he saw the four men emerge from the side street between the bank building and the Victory — closer to the bank. And in an instant, even from a little distance, he could see that this was Burnham and his three compadres.

York climbed down and drew his gun, and then it came to him he was inside a shop with its front double doors locked, and cursed his stupidity for not thinking of that. He was kicking those doors open when a shotgun blast sounded up the street, luckily concealing the wood giving way under his boot, and when he got to the street he could make out a ghostlike figure in the window on the second floor of the bank building . . .

. . . Jonathan P. Tulley in his hospital gown with a shotgun in his hands, angled downward.

And in the street, facedown — or body down, because no face was left to speak of, just some neck pouring red into the white

— was one of Burnham's boys, while their leader and the other two were milling in momentary panic. One was scooping snow up to wash the gore from his face.

Then Burnham cried, *"Moody! Forget that! Get that son of a bitch!"*

And Tulley left the window while one of Burnham's boys ran back around the side of the bank building, while the other two headed York's way. Even from where York stood, the heavy footsteps going up the side exterior stairs to Doc Miller's office could easily be heard, like drumbeats.

With Moody Fender dispatched to take care of whoever it was that had ambushed them, blowing Jake Warlow's head clean off (well, not *clean* off), Ned Sivley and Luke Burnham ran as best they could through the deep snow drifting across Main Street. Running in sand would have been swifter.

The boss was at Sivley's side, saying, "We'll get the horses at Maxwell's and light out!"

Sivley said nothing, trying to suppress a cough.

Then somebody over at the left was running right for them, down the boardwalk, which was cleared enough to make his passage quicker than theirs. Somebody in a black frock coat and black hat, the coat flapping like the wings of an angry swooping raven, the hat flying off like a smaller black bird, and a big handgun pointed right at them.

Could that be . . . *Caleb York?*

Burnham thought so, apparently, because he stopped in his tracks and screamed, *"Caleb York!"* and fired right at the man, who dropped to the boardwalk and fired back.

The bullet took Sivley down, through the chest, and he fell backward, sending up bursts of powdery snow; the lunger lay there, looking up at the white-swirling gray of a sky that seemed to have no sun in it at all, snowflakes kissing his face, then he started to cough blood, but the liquid caught in his throat and gathered in his mouth and he began choking and drowning in bubbling scarlet. He was still in the process of dying when a second shot from the prone shooter on the boardwalk knocked Burnham back and down, arms spread, like a kid making a snow angel.

Caleb York got up, a man in black with the front of him coated white, then ran over bareheaded to the two bodies with his .44 extended and ready. He kicked each man's gun away. Sivley was kind of gargling blood, and would be gone in seconds or maybe minutes. Burnham was either unconscious or dead, his face to one side, the milky eye shut. The bullet appeared to be a chest wound near his left shoulder. Whether the outlaw was breathing or not could not be told, the duster too bulky and concealing to know without stopping for inspection. Burnham had a big canvas bank bag slung over his left arm. York didn't bother with that for now.

He could take no more time with these fallen outlaws — not when he knew the remaining one had been dispatched to deal with Tulley. He ran as well as the Main Street accumulation of white would allow, and soon was going up the stairs, fast, to the landing outside Doc Miller's office.

The door hadn't been locked, so York went right in, much as Moody Fender no doubt had. The office was empty, and so was the surgery. The sitting room off of which the bedrooms lay was also empty, though heavy tracks of snowy footprints led, not surprisingly, to the sickroom.

An unearthly scream came from behind the closed door to that room.

York shouldered in and there stood the sullen outlaw, covered in dripping yellow liquid, beads of it dangling from his hat brim, his eyes wide, his expression horrified. He had a Merwin .38 in hand; he was facing the overturned sickbed, which had been pushed on its side to make a barrier by Tulley, the top of whose head could just barely be seen by York. The drenched outlaw, his face a mask of rage, swung toward the sheriff, who put a bullet in the man's chest.

Moody Fender's last word was, "Shit," before he collapsed in a pile of dead, a patient Dr. Miller would have no luck reviving. The outlaw's last word was inaccurate, because as Tulley popped up from behind the barricade of his sickbed, he was holding in both hands, as if it were a serving dish, the now empty chamber pot, the contents of which he'd splashed on his would-be assailant.

Tulley seemed embarrassed. " 'twas all I had at hand," he said. "I used up both barrels of the scattergun, blowin' that other fool's head offen his shoulders."

Whether by "other fool," Tulley referred to himself or the urine-drenched dead outlaw between them on the floor, remained open to interpretation.

York took only time to smile before he rushed out to check on the other two bodies.

But only one body awaited him.
Burnham was gone.

But only one body awaited him.

Burnham was gone.

CHAPTER TEN

Seeing the skinny lunger sprawled dead on the snow-covered street, without the outlaw leader lying next to him, Caleb York realized he had not killed Burnham, merely wounded him. Somehow the bastard had managed to get up again and stagger off.

But in which direction?

York went over and retrieved his hat, putting it on with his left hand while keeping his right filled with the .44. He looked up and down Main, his detective's eyes searching through snow that still came down, if not quite so heavily.

The drifted street was stirred between where York stood and the saddle shop half a block behind him, the result of both the outlaws and himself heading to the bank from Maxwell's. Beyond the bank, looking toward the east, he clearly saw plenty more of the white stuff disturbed by the many footsteps of customers who'd headed into the Victory from all up and down the street.

The other day, Rita had told York that while the cowboys who'd chosen the saloon as their oasis in the storm were staying put, other locals — going stir-crazy, fighting cabin fever — would head over to the Victory, time to time, for drinks and some food.

So that meant the outlaw had ceded to the snow no tracks that stood out from the rest . . . unless he'd left a blood trail. But Burnham's bleeding must have soaked into his clothing under the duster, because no red stood out on the white, except what the dead lunger had spilled and, of course, where the one outlaw had lost his head.

York half smiled at his own grisly if unintentional joke.

Where had the son of a bitch Burnham gone?

Had the raider broken into one of the stores, perhaps through the back, to seek warmth and shelter and try not to bleed to death? Or was Burnham thinking more of revenge than survival, hoping York would come looking for him and walk into a bullet, or two or six?

The most logical possibility — the nearest shelter that the outlaw might possibly have reached before a blood trail began — was the saddle shop. Not the shop itself, but the second-floor living quarters where the haul from the Vegas bank job had been waiting — possibly, if Burnham's wound allowed, for him to retrieve it before fleeing.

Of course, right now that haul wasn't where the gang had put it, even if it was still in the shop — York had left the saddlebags he'd filled with the loot on the back of the saddle stand.

More pertinent, though, were the horses waiting in the workshop at the rear of the building with its several stable stalls. If he were Burnham, that's where he'd head — hop a horse and get somewhere else, fast as the weather allowed.

But frustrating as it was, York had to take it slow. He knew Burnham was likely lying in wait for him, so rushing through the late Maxwell's little world of living quarters and commerce could have fatal consequences for the sheriff.

So he started with the shop, going in low through the front doors he'd kicked open not long ago. With no lamps lit, the place was shadowed even by day — it was afternoon now — and York took his time, moving on his haunches.

The shop was empty, the saddlebags of money still riding the stand behind the saddle where earlier York had perched. So at least that hadn't been found.

Again keeping low, York and his .44 moved into the workshop, where he found the two horses still in their stalls. No sign a thing had been touched since he checked here earlier. Nor did the cramped sleeping quarters of the absent Mexican saddle maker show any signs that someone had been here since York.

Who now had a decision to make. Go up the back steps to the apartment, where Burnham could well be waiting at the top of the stairwell for the sheriff to emerge. Or go back outside and up the exterior staircase and in where the outlaw waited, ready to shoot him dead.

York decided on the stairwell, where he'd left the door open up top. Outside, he would be exposed to too many possibilities for ambush — corners for Burnham to hide behind, rooftops to pick York off from, windows to shoot at him from. Going up the steps, confined though he'd be, the dangers were real but predictable.

After getting out of the frock coat, York rested it and his hat on top of a display case. This left him in his light gray shirt with black string tie and his black cotton pants. His boots he slipped off, anticipating exploring the apartment above, where his stocking feet wouldn't announce him.

Staying low, gun angled upward, his back to the wall of the well, York slowly ascended. He paused at each step and listened. Then, one step down from the top, he pitched himself through the open doorway, sliding in flat on his belly with his gun aimed up and ready.

The hallway was empty.

So was the indoor privy at the end of it, and the two facing bedrooms. Slow and careful, he made his exploration, pausing frequently to listen.

Nothing.

And that is what he found in the kitchen and the living room. Everything, including the dirty dishes and cups on the table, was as he'd left it. He pushed through the door he'd kicked open earlier to check the landing now, and it too was free of anything but the snow still piling up out there. Fresh accumulation on the stairs to the street seemed undisturbed.

Back down in the shadows of the saddle shop, York again got into his frock coat, hat, and boots, frowning. He'd guessed wrong. The close proximity of the saddle shop had seemed the most likely destination for the wounded outlaw, where Burnham could have taken a horse and checked on his money, if he was inclined to leave town. Or to set up an ambush within the living quarters for Caleb York when the sheriff came around.

Neither had proved true.

Lost in thought, he returned to the bodies in the snow-drifted street.

Burnham, he knew, was shrewd. The man had seen York coming from the direction of the saddle shop and likely instantly figured that the Vegas bank money was lost, and possibly the horses had been slapped on the ass and sent running, or maybe killed by York.

York, of course, would never have considered killing the animals to keep the outlaws from using them. But the one-time guerilla raider wouldn't have thought twice before putting bullets in the brains of the beasts. So he'd assumed the same of York.

Where *had* the outlaw gone?

The possibility that Burnham had holed up in one of the closed stores, breaking in to do so, couldn't be ignored. But checking each of them would take precious time — if Burnham was fleeing on horseback, in whatever direction, the outlaw would be getting a hell of a head start.

What to do first? What to do next?

"If I were ye," Deputy Jonathan P. Tulley

said, "I would see if that there banker feller is alive or dead inside of that bank of hissen."

This voice might have been in York's imagination, conjuring what Tulley would have thought in reply. While it did sometimes seem that old desert rat *could* read York's mind, what was more surprising right now was the deputy's presence in the street next to him.

Yet there Tulley stood, no longer in his hospital gown, rather in a heavy black jacket that York recognized as one of Doc Miller's, and the dark flannel shirt, gray woolen pants, and red suspenders he'd worn the night he was shot — just a few days ago! The deputy probably wore the usual work boots, too, but those were buried in the snow where he stood, bandy-legged and bright-eyed.

"What the hell," York said, "are you doing out of bed?"

"Wal, sir, that bed got all upended, like . . . and that sickroom of mine has a dead man in it with his brains spilled out, and I believe he soiled hisself upon dyin'. Plus which, in addition, the place reeks like some damn horse pissed all over it."

"That's not a horse's work, Tulley. It's yours." York shook his head. "I can't believe

230

the doc approved this."

"Wal, he didn't. He's still out 'n' about, tryin' to save people's noses and toes-es and fingers and such, that been bit up by the frost. Me, I feel fine, but not fine enough to put that bed back the way she belongs, plus I don't cotton to spendin' time with no dead man what did his business in his britches."

York looked at Tulley.

Tulley looked at York.

"Sheriff," the deputy said. "I am rarin' to go. Tell me how I can best be of use to ye."

Truth was, Tulley *could* be of use.

"Right now," York said, "we go over and see how that bank president fared."

A big smile blossomed. "You're followin' *my* counsel!"

"I am following your counsel, yes. Now, Tulley, if you feel tired or faint, you just let me know. Don't be shy."

"Ain't never been accused of bein' the shy type."

"No. I would imagine not."

They trudged through the snow to the bank, skirting dead outlaws. The front doors were locked and they went around back where, though fresh snow had filled it in somewhat, the area the robbers had cleared away with their feet by the door was still evident.

Shortly the sheriff and his deputy were inside and freeing the bank president, York getting his ivory-handled Sheffield folding knife from his right-hand pants pocket to cut the twine binding the man. The banker thanked them and York quickly questioned him.

Godfrey, who was still sitting on the floor with the two lawmen hunkered down around him, finished up his story by saying, "I heard what I took for a shotgun blast outside. Was anyone injured?"

Tulley said, "I blowed the head offen one of 'em."

Godfrey frowned. "Which one?"

York said, "Not the leader, who I wounded but got away. The skinny one I killed, and I plugged the stupid-looking one, too. I saw the whole bunch of 'em together at the Victory a few days ago — I think it was the handsome fella that Tulley sent to hell."

The banker shook his head. "Too bad."

York frowned. "Pardon?"

Godfrey sighed. "I believe that man saved my life. He outright talked the others into not killing me. On the other hand, I feel sure the one heading up the gang is a ruthless, heartless killer."

"You're not wrong."

York helped the man to his feet.

Godfrey asked, "What do I do now?"

"We'll check the upstairs," York said, "and make sure it's safe for you to stay there . . . unless you'd rather go to the hotel, or perhaps a table at the Victory?"

The little banker waved a hand. "No, no. My apartment will be fine. As far as what happened here, I will deal with that tomorrow, when my . . . my head is clear."

"Fine."

"If I understood you right, all those men have met their Maker except for the leader."

"Yes. Lucas Burnham. He was one of Quantrill's top lieutenants. Quantrill's Raiders?"

"Oh my," the banker said, his lips against his fingers. "I'm glad I answered as I did."

"Answered what?"

"His question about where I hailed from. I said Kentucky. Not true, but I said it."

"Good choice," York said, and grinned and patted the man's shoulder. "I believe Raymond Parker made a good choice, too — in you."

"Thank you, sir."

Tulley stayed with the banker while York went outside and up the stairs to the third-floor living quarters. The place was clear of any threat.

With the banker locked in at home, York

and Tulley came down the exterior stairs, where Doc Miller — looking confused, worried, and a little irritated — was coming up.

They met on the second-floor landing, wind whipping white around them as if they stood inside a snow globe.

"What's this?" the doctor demanded. "Corpses in the street and Tulley out of bed? Is this your handiwork, Caleb?"

"Some of it. The one with the haircut that got a mite too close is my deputy's doing."

Tulley was nodding. "Me and the scatter-gun. Uh, Doc, you best be wary. There's a mess in my sickroom."

"Is that right?"

Tulley nodded. "A chamber pot got spilled. Also some blood and innards."

The doc didn't shock easily and it was almost amusing to see his eyes go that wide and his mouth drop that far open. But right there on the landing in the falling snow, York explained and the doc calmed.

"Well, Tulley," Miller said, "we need to straighten up in there and get you back in bed."

"No, sir. I done checked out of this horse-pitul."

York said, "Tulley's right. I need him. These are obviously extraordinary circumstances and I can use his help. If he shows

signs of failing, I will ship him back to you."
The doc smirked. "Not in a wicker casket, I hope."

"No, but speaking of wicker caskets, could you call on our undertaker friend, Perkins, and get those bodies off the street and that one out of your quarters? You should also check in with the bank president, Peter Godfrey — he got some rough treatment from the brigands. Freshen up first, if you like."

"You're too good to me, Caleb."

"Well, now that you're the official coroner of the city of Trinidad, it *is* your job."

"It is at that," the doctor admitted, then nodded and went inside with a sigh.

At the bottom of the steps, Tulley turned to York and said, "I forgot my scattergun! It's upstairs!"

The deputy was starting back up, but York stopped him with a hand on an arm. "It's also empty. Go help yourself to a gun off one of the dead men. Get yourself a cartridge belt, too."

Tulley had started nodding in the middle of that, seeing the wisdom of the sheriff's words. Soon he was putting on the gun belt that had once belonged to the dead lunger.

York explained to his deputy that Burnham might be holed up in one of the shops, and — if so — had likely broken in, in back.

"So you go behind the shops on the south side of Main," York said, "and I'll take the north side, in back, looking for signs of a break-in. Tulley, if you see such signs, don't go . . ." He almost said "blundering," but instead said, "roaring in. Come find me and we'll handle it together."

"Yes, sir."

"We'll end up at the jail. If there's been no sign of Burnham breaking in anywhere, we check the livery stable."

Tulley nodded again. "Ye figure he mighta took a horse from the livery."

"Yes. But it does seem a bit unlikely, since he was closer to the horses at Maxwell's. A wounded man beating a path to the livery, all the way to the west end of Main, when he had a better option? Well, that doesn't make much sense to me."

"I guess. Iffen he weren't a military man."

York frowned. "What's that, Deputy?"

Tulley shrugged. "This Burn 'Em feller, he ran with Quantrill. He thinks half sojer, half raider. I think first he saw that *you* was 'tween him and them horses at Maxwell's. Now, I *know* he wants a crack at ye, Caleb York, for past indignities . . . but not when ye got the advantage! Not when this feller is shot to hell and just wants to live through it."

"In which case," York said, heading over to the boardwalk, Tulley working to keep up, "he would make straight for the livery."

They were walking side by side now, and the boardwalk was cleared enough, if spottily, to make the going better than in the drifted street. Also, the overhang lessened the falling snow.

"And this Burn 'Em feller," Tulley said, "he *knows* how you think, Caleb York. He knows you ain't no military man. Ye be Wells Fargo, a detective, and you'd search the town one end to the tother. Might even be smart enough to figger you might rule out him a-fleein' on horseback, since he didn't go back for an animal at Maxwell's. Might figger you'd think him wantin' revenge so dang bad would keep him in town. So, meanin' no awful fence, this here feller may have out-thunk you, Sheriff. Like I say, meanin' no awful fence."

"Tulley," York said, walking as quick as the snow on the boardwalk would allow, "when did you get so damn smart?"

"I was always this smart," he said. "I went purt' near to the end of third grade. My maw said I was the smartest of us boys."

"How many of you boys were there?"

"Two."

They made the trek to the east end of Main Street in not much more time than it would have taken in normal weather. They paused on the porch outside the jailhouse office. Off to their right, at the dead end of Main, was the livery stable. Directly across from them was the little barrio, which the sheriff nodded toward.

"If Burnham hasn't left town," York said, "he very well could be dug in over there. Wouldn't be hard for him to take over one of those huts from a family and wait for me to walk by or stick my head in."

"The cantina," Tulley said, gesturing in that direction, "with them rooms up top for the angels what fell up there? That be a fine place to relax while waitin' to kill some feller."

York smiled at that, but he didn't dispute it. Then he said, "Go in and get another scattergun for yourself. Bring plenty of shells."

"Yes, sir," Tulley said, and did that.

On his deputy's return, York said, "I'll take the livery in front and you take the back."

"Yes, sir."

"Don't do anything unless you hear a gunshot or till I call for you. You hear a shot, then bust in and, if I'm not standing, take the son of a bitch down."

Tulley's nod was firm. "I'll take the damn head right offen him."

York nodded. "Seems to be your style."

Tulley grinned. Apparently this was the first he'd heard he had a style.

Double doors for riding a horse in or out were on either side of the barnlike building, but at the right of them, both front and back, was a regular door. Normally the double doors in front stood open, but they were shut in this unfriendly weather. The building itself, a weathered gray wooden structure that looked like this wind might take it down, wore a snowy hat on its gabled roof.

York, .44 Colt in hand, approached slowly as Tulley headed around to the other side. Pausing at the double doors, which would open outward, he considered using the normal-size entry.

Then he reconsidered.

He yanked open the big door at right, not all the way, just enough for him to dive in and to the left, which he did, landing on straw. On his back, looking up, he fanned the .44 around, but no one was standing except the many horses, some of whom whinnied at his entrance. He waited to see if Burnham would pop up from among the horses, and his eyes searched through their skinny legs for any trousers among them.

No.

Then, as he got to his feet, York saw him.

Not Burnham, but Lem Hansen, the bulky blacksmith, sprawled on the floor just outside an improbably empty stall. York went to him quickly, while looking all around to see if Burnham was lying in wait. A killer might be ready to ambush the sheriff, if York were distracted by the fallen stable man, who was not dead; Hansen was not even unconscious, simply moaning and bloodied along the back of his head.

No sign of Burnham, though, and after several moments, York helped Hansen up into a sitting position. The blacksmith sat with his hands limp in the lap of his leather apron.

"What happened here, Lem?"

Hansen, groggy, his eyes half-lidded, said, "He . . . he been shot. Had a gun in his hand. Wanted the bes' horse."

"Sure he did," York said. "He wanted the most rested, fastest horse stabled here."

"He did," the blacksmith confirmed.

And the place was jammed with horse-flesh, the heating stove putting out nicely. York was relieved his gelding was still in its stall.

York said, "Did he offer to pay?"

"He . . . he offered to trade . . . two horses. For one. Said they was in the workshop, 'hind the saddle shop. I said . . . said, I can't trade you or sell you a horse that ain't mine. Most of these is just kept here for the storm."

York nodded toward the nearby empty stall. "So he stuck that gun in your ribs and made you show him to the best horse."

The blacksmith started to shake his head, then thought better of it. "Happened jus' 'bout like that. I give him Mr. Mathers's bes' horse . . . personal mount. And he give me . . . give me . . ."

"Gave you that clout on the head, didn't he, Lem?"

"He did. He did at that. Seen him afore . . . slept here few nights back."

"Had a milky eye, didn't he?"

"He did! Scar runnin' through it. Smiled some but weren't nothin' about smilin' in that there smile."

"Understood."

"He was weavin' some . . . wounded how bad, I can't say. Me, I don't feel so good myself."

"I'll get you some help. . . . *Tulley!*"

Tulley came in, loaded for bear, scatter-gun sweeping all around. Then he came

241

over, threading through the milling horses, getting some neighs but no yays. The old boy crouched next to the blacksmith, who sat on the hay with his legs straight out like a child playing jacks, the sheriff kneeling nearby.

"Deputy," York said, "fetch Doc Miller. He may be busy with the undertaker or he might be visiting Mr. Godfrey. But find him and tell him we have a live patient for him for a change."

"Yes, sir," Tulley said with a nod, and went off, finding his way through the cluster of horses.

As the deputy was going, York called, "If I'm not here when you get back, I'm out after Burnham!"

"Yes, sir!"

"You watch the town for me!"

"Like a gol' dang *hawk*!"

Tulley slipped out the front double doors, closed them behind him.

York said, "Any other talk between you and the milky-eyed man?"

"S-some. He wanted to know where the nearest shelter was. I said, north or south? He said north. I said, probably the Brentwood Junction relay station. I said he could eat there, mos' likely, even though the stagecoaches ain't runnin'. He wanted to know how far, and I said normal weather, half hour. He asked if there was any place closer. I said, not open to the public. He said, what about *not* open to the public. I said, just the Bar-O."

York frowned. "You mentioned the Bar-O?"

"Afraid so. He said, ain't that the Cullen place? I said it was. He said, ain't that run by a girl? I said that was so. He said, ain't she suppose to be sweet on Caleb York? And I said, such things ain't my business."

The hair on the back of York's neck was standing up. "And what did he say next?"

"Nothing. He just whacked me on the head with the butt of his pistol."

The blacksmith's eyes were drooping. York had questioned him hard, probably too hard. He moved the man just a shade, to where he could lean back against the wooden side of a stall.

York stood. "Thank you, Lem. You rest. Doc'll be here soon."

"S-sorry, Sheriff."

"No need."

"Shouldn't have tol' him of the Bar-O."

"No. You shouldn't have."

But the blacksmith was asleep, and York was getting his dappled gelding out of its stall and saddled up. He had to ride out into this storm one last time.

CHAPTER ELEVEN

Willa Cullen sat on the hearth of the stone fireplace beside a snapping, crackling fire in the living room of the ranch house, feeling very alone. Though lamps on small tables glowed yellow in two windows, the long, rather narrow room with its mix of her mother's fine furnishings and her father's rustic creations was mostly unlighted.

The fire threw flickering reflections on the young woman, who — in her red-and-black plaid shirt and jeans and boots — felt not at all feminine right now. She had no idea how lovely she looked, half-turned toward the warmth and flames in a pensive posture, highlighted in shimmering soft orange and deep blue shadows.

Her sense of aloneness was more a literal feeling than an emotional one, as everyone else on the ranch house grounds was out dealing with the realities of this stubborn storm — even plump Harmon had traded his cookhouse for a saddle. The bunkhouse was empty and stable man Lou Morgan had been recruited into the small army on horseback to help deal with scattered, stranded cattle and cowhands who were out there somewhere in the drifting snow and hadn't been heard from for too long.

"I'll keep an eye on the horse barn," she assured Lou, before he joined the effort.

"Much obliged, Miz Cullen. Keep that heat stove stoked. Critters'll ketch their death if you don't."

"I will, and they'll get plenty of oats and hay, too."

She'd watched them ride off and disappear into the wall of white. Willa only hoped the undertaking would help, and wouldn't just add more names to the list of the missing.

Icy flakes pelted the windows and whipping wind shook the porch beams and rails in an unrelenting reminder that the blizzard still ruled the land. Despite the warmth of the fire, she hugged her arms to herself, fighting a chill that was more mental than physical. She wondered if the Bar-O would survive this onslaught by Nature.

Had she done everything she could?

Willa tried to imagine what her father might have done differently, knowing too

well that George Cullen would have preferred a son, though both her late parents
had encouraged her to be feminine *and*
strong.

When she turned away from the fire, she
could just see Papa seated there in the
nearby rough-hewn chair he'd fashioned
himself — though carpentry had been a
necessity not a passion of his, a skill learned
by doing. The Papa her memory summoned
had eyes bright and seeing. Not the blind
old man whose orbs were a spooky white.
Smoking a pipe, his expression peaceful,
not judgmental at all, this Papa seemed to
reassure her without a word, his expression
saying, *Man can only do so much, daughter.
God will have His way.*

Not "a man," but "man" — the human
race. That she was female had never been
something Papa had held over her. However
much he might have liked to have a son.

She thought, too, of Caleb York. Though
she felt no guilt for taking him into her bed,
she wondered if this man — a man she
seemed unable to stop loving — would ever
be able to bring himself to join her here at
the Bar-O. If not, could she go with him,
wherever he led her? *Whither though goest,*
the Bible said, *I will go.* But that was a

woman talking to another woman, wasn't it?

Living in a town like Trinidad, or a city like San Diego, seemed a foreign concept to her. She liked Denver, adored Denver really, but to visit — for the fine hotels and restaurants and the amusements. Living day to day in such a place as a married woman . . . raising children, cooking meals for the family, mending and sewing, doing the housework? None of these things had she ever seriously considered. True, she did some of these things here, but also, so much more. . . .

Now, if Caleb were willing to live out here, and help her run the Bar-O, with enough money rolling in to hire help for cooking and cleaning and maybe a governess for the kids . . .

What kids?

And for that matter, after the blizzard, what Bar-O?

A knocking at the door startled her out of solitude. Might be her foreman, Earl Colson, with a report. Could even be Caleb, making a return visit. The latter made her smile, then frown, then smile again. Still, it seemed somehow a surprise that anyone else could even exist out here.

When she opened the door, the figure

standing before her was neither her foreman nor Caleb, but a duster-garbed
stranger. Broad-shouldered, as big as the
sheriff, and just as impressive, even if he
seemed barely able to keep on his feet — he
even had to lean a gloved hand against the
door frame for support. His battered black
hat hung heavy with snow, and tiny icicles
clung to his bearded face, his eyes all but
closed. His duster wore a coating of white,
giving him a ghostly look, disrupted only by
an iced-over patch of scarlet on his chest
near his shoulder, which spoke of a bullet
wound.

"Ma'am," he said, in a voice touched by
the South, "I am a weary traveler in trouble.
Might I impose upon your kindness?"

She did not reply, just put her arm around
his shoulder — the one not close to the
probable wound — and walked him inside.
She closed the door and he leaned against
it as she took his hat and helped him out of
the duster, then hung them on the wall
hooks.

Oddly, he wore an ancient Confederate
officer's jacket, the black blood-crusted hole
in which confirmed he'd suffered a bullet
wound. He wore a gun belt, which he
started to take off, perhaps to show he was
no threat to her; but when he seemed about

to lose his balance, she helped him with it, and hung it on a hook, too.

Willa guided him through the living room, leaving behind him a melting trail of winter weather. Getting to the pair of rough-wood chairs near the fireplace and its warmth took a while, though he did not stumble. He grimaced yet neither moaned nor groaned when she settled him down.

"You've been shot," she said.

For the first time he opened his eyes, and she saw that he had a scar that ran vertically through the center of his left eye, which was now a milky white. She almost gasped — not because it was disturbing, but because it brought her own father's sightless eyes back to mind.

"We need," she said, "to get you out of that jacket."

He nodded and extended his arms crucifixion-style, grimacing again but making no sound. She slipped the garment off him and folded it, then set it aside on the floor.

He rasped, "I . . . I'll want that back."

She smiled. "I have no use for it. Sit forward. Just enough for me to get a look at the back of you."

He did, and she had her look and said, "Appears to be an exit wound. Bullet went

250

through you. You're lucky."

"Am I?"

She gave him a smile. "Some stupid physician won't be sticking his dirty fingers in your wound, and then trying to dig out the bullet with some unsterilized thingamajig. When this storm subsides, we'll get Dr. Miller out here from town — you may not realize it, but you're near Trinidad — to have a look at you."

He seemed to be struggling to stay conscious. "I . . . I was heading there. I put up at that way station when the storm got bad. Comin' from Las Vegas."

"Don't talk. Can you get out of that shirt, while I gather some things?"

He swallowed, nodded. The fire was reflecting off his face, the snow and ice that had encrusted his beard starting to melt into what might be mistaken for tears.

When she came back his shirt was off, and tossed onto the jacket. He had a decent, sinewy build, but much bullet scarred. From the war that his jacket spoke of, she wondered? Otherwise, what kind of life was her guest leading, to come to a strange house seeking shelter with a bullet wound?

No time for questions or answers now.

The bullet had gone in small but came out bigger; however, the cold had helped clot both entry and exit. When the warmth of the house and this fireplace thawed him, maybe the clotting would go, which wouldn't help matters.

Willa warmed water on the kitchen stove and gathered towels, bandages, and a bottle of her father's Old Crow whiskey from a cupboard shelf. Soon she had cleaned up her patient and given him a drink from the bottle before applying the alcohol to the wounds, fore and aft. This time he did make a little noise. She could not blame him.

In perhaps ten minutes, she had him bandaged, wrapping the gauze around his torso, then helped her patient back into the shirt. He was studying her; that one milky eye did not bother her as it would have some people. She had sympathy for him, left over from her father.

"You are . . . you're a kind woman," he said, as if he'd just spotted some rare species in the wild.

"Even today," she said, shrugging, kneeling next to him, "this is hard country. People have to help each other out."

"Not all do. From where do your people hail?"

She pointed to the floor. "I hail from right here. I was born in this house. My father lived many places. Ohio, mostly. So. Have I earned the right to ask the circumstances of your wound?"

His expression darkened, his eyes gazing past her. "I came upon . . . I came upon some rabble who were in the act of stealing a buckboard wagon . . . from a father and son. They . . . your tender ears may not wish to hear. . . ."

"I grew up on this ranch. I've seen kindness and cruelty and everything between. Don't spare my feelings in telling your story."

She, of course, could not know that the real story from which Lucas Burnham wove his lies was crueler still.

"I attempted," he said, "to stop it, but I was . . . I was *one* man, and they were four of the lowest kind. The man and his son were killed."

She recoiled. "How terrible."

He shook his head as if he couldn't believe what some men were capable of. "*Most* terrible. I shot and, I believe, killed two of the four, but was wounded myself . . . as you know . . . and I rode away into the thick of the storm . . . where they dare not follow."

Something about her patient's stilted language warned her, finally, that she had made a mistake. What she had taken as a certain gentlemanly formality now seemed perhaps contrived. She wasn't certain of it, but an alarm bell was ringing, however faintly.

She rose and gathered the enameled tin of water she'd brought from the kitchen, bloody towels wadded within, then offered him one more swig of the Old Crow. He took the offer, smiled, and said, "Thank you, ma'am," then handed it back.

"Let's get you back into your shirt."

She crouched to help him. Again, his grimaces were not accompanied by moans or groans. He was a brave soldier.

"You just rest there now," she said, rising.

"What is your name, child?"

With the bowl in her arms, she said with a smile, "You must make up your mind, sir. Am I 'ma'am' or 'child'?"

"As a gracious hostess, you're a 'ma'am.' With your youth and beauty, a child."

"And you are?"

Something proud came into his expression. "I am Luke Burnham. Have you heard that name before?"

"No. Should I have?"

"Possibly. I made something out of it during the war . . . but that was likely before you were born. I've told you my name. What is yours?"

"Willa Cullen. This is the Bar-O where

you find yourself stranded. One of the largest spreads around these parts, although after this blizzard finishes with us, there may not be much of anything of value left in this Territory, big *or* small."

"I never saw the like," he said, shaking his head, then glancing toward the iced-over windows, the howl of wind proving his point. "Something else I never saw the like of."

"Yes?"

"Your kindness. Ma'am. Child." He smiled and it was almost charming.

Willa returned the smile, somewhat, wondering whether she should be scared or comforted.

She took everything back into the kitchen, dumping the water in the sink, leaving the bloody towels on the counter, then putting the whiskey bottle away in a cupboard.

When she came back, her guest was asleep. She took the Indian blanket from the other chair by the fire and covered him up with it. He was breathing deep. With that wound, a bed might have done him better, but she did not want to disturb him.

Willa returned to the hearth, near the warmth of the dancing flames, but kept her eyes on her guest. In these last few minutes that alarm bell had begun to ring louder.

255

That milky eye that had made her think of her father was no longer warming, like this fire. Rather, it made her study the scar that ran through his eye, the physical reminder, and remainder, of violence in this man's past, like the scars on his flesh.

The sound of a horse whinnying in discomfort was not loud enough to wake her guest, but made Willa realize that she had been so quick to help the distressed traveler she found on her doorstep, to bring him inside, to warm him and bind his wounds, that she hadn't given one thought to how he got here. The frosted-over windows were no use, so she went to the door and looked out. A black horse, a very handsome steed, was tied out front.

The poor creature would freeze if she didn't act quickly.

She got into her brown woolen box coat with its three ulster-like capes, snugged on leather gloves, tugged on a fur-trimmed matching bonnet, and went out to brave the storm. The horse, tied at the rail just past the porch, was dancing against the cold, trying to shake the ice and snow off its mane and tail; she approached and calmed it with a hand on its muzzle and her voice in its ear, with the intention of unhitching the animal and walking it by the bridle over to the horse barn.

Something about the animal seemed familiar. Didn't Clarence Mathers, the hardware store owner, have a Morgan horse like this? She checked the brand, which was indeed CMH, the *H* for hardware.

That was when she noticed the large canvas bag slung over the horse, between the front of the saddle and the rise of the steed's long neck. She took a closer look at the bag, but didn't have to open it to guess its contents.

The feel of the smaller coin and cash bags within the larger one made that clear enough, and the stenciled words FIRST BANK OF TRINIDAD confirmed her assumption.

The man with the bullet wound and the milky eye was a bank robber and a horse thief. Not some Good Samaritan who had tried unsuccessfully to rescue a father and son . . .

On the rump of the animal, in back of the saddle, was a rifle scabbard. In it was a Winchester Lever Action 1873, a weapon well-known to a girl who grew up on a ranch. She withdrew it from its home and checked to see if it was loaded.

It was.

She swallowed. Girded herself and turned

with the rifle in hand, toward the nearby steps to the porch. She took her first step in that direction when the front door opened, freezing her, her guest silhouetted against the light of the indoors. His features were lost in shadow, but when he brought up his hand, the steel of the revolver in it flashed before he fired.

CHAPTER TWELVE

Wolves or coyotes had got to them.

The bodies of the father and son, whose buckboard Caleb York had discovered behind the saddle-shop building, had been dug up and dined upon, two human beings turned into slaughterhouse leavings on the roadside. The grisly sight was softened only slightly by subsequent snowfall giving them a dignified dusting.

York barely paused to take in the grotesque evidence of deaths caused by far worse predators than those who had feasted here. Recovery of what remained of the man and boy would wait for the storm to end and the sun to reveal other terrible secrets.

The sheriff could not spare time in the already painfully slow pursuit of Lucas Burnham, who almost certainly was making his way to the Bar-O and Willa Cullen. Astride his faithful dappled gray gelding, York was busy riding through and around the shifting, drifting snow on that road north, defined only by telegraph poles, themselves heavy with white, lines sagging with ice.

Black frock coat flapping, hat tied down with a muffler, another woolen scarf wrapped around his face, leaving little but his eyes exposed, York leaned into the hungry wind and eddying snow, a dark wraith flying through an afternoon that seemed as impenetrable as any night. Yet he took care not to push the gelding too hard. If the animal died underneath him, should an ankle snap in deep snow, should its great heart burst, the rider would be marooned on this bleached beach with his goal unreachable.

He could not know Burnham's intentions. Possibly the man — that word didn't seem to cover it, perhaps "fiend" was more like it — sought to strike back at York by defiling or doing Willa in, or both. Or perhaps the fiend's own human needs — the wound that needed doctoring, the shelter required in this hellish storm — had sent him to the Bar-O as the nearest safe haven.

And why not? What better than to wait in a warm ranch house for the object of your revenge to deliver himself?

Caleb York was not an overly emotional

man. He felt things deep but tended to hold them in, hardly unusual among his contemporaries, particularly those who had chosen the unforgiving West for their home. But within him roiled rage and dread, as he contemplated the inevitability of Lucas Burnham reaching the Cullen ranch before him.

Forty minutes had dragged themselves by before the Bar-O's rough-wood log arch materialized off to the right, the plaque swaying in the wind, swinging hard enough to shake off any snow that might otherwise have clung. Still, the flurries themselves seemed to have lessened some, as York on the gelding swung into the turn where the dirt lane lay buried somewhere beneath the animal's hoofbeats, as they churned up powdery bursts.

As before, the buildings of the Bar-O appeared like an illusory image and not the reality, a crystalline suggestion aswirl in ivory flecks of the ranch house and its outbuildings. As he drew nearer, coming in past a corral gathering only frozen precipitation, York could make out a slight figure in shades of brown standing beside a fine black horse that he knew belonged to Trinidad's hardware man.

Willa!

What was she doing? She was alongside the horse, doing something . . . taking a rifle from the scabbard alongside the saddle, and then turning toward the house, where the front door opened and a figure — *could that be Burnham?* — fired at her, making small, awful thunder in this frigid gale.

She went down!

But she was moving from her prone position on her belly, firing back twice, creating two more small thunder cracks in the vocal weather, and the door slammed.

Near the ranch house, York slid off the still moving gelding and, .44 in his gloved hand now, slow-ran through the deep snow to the woman on the ground, her back to him, propped up barely on her elbows. He knelt by her and she looked up at him, the pretty face framed by the fur-trimmed brown bonnet, pink flesh sprinkled with snow. Her eyes widened and her smiling expression was a girlish thing, surprised and delighted.

"Are you hit?" he asked, breathless.

"No! No, I'm fine. Is the horse all right?"

That was so like her.

"It's fine." He helped her to her feet, but said, "Stay low. He could be at a window."

They hunkered.

She asked, "Who *is* he?"

"Lucas Burnham."

"That's the name he gave. Meant nothing to me. He seemed almost proud of it."

"Oh, he *is* proud." York didn't tell her she'd likely be dead now had she recognized it. " 'Burn 'Em' Burnham rode with Quantrill. He's a butcher." He had her elbow now. "Let's walk our animals to the stable."

Her cornflower-blue eyes were wild as an alley cat's. "We should go in after him! I don't want him burning *me* out!"

"I don't think that's what he has in mind. What you're going to do is go into that horse barn with your rifle. If he circles around, comes in and tries for a horse, shoot him in the head."

"My pleasure."

They walked the animals, the hardware store horse on the outside, York and Willa between it and the gelding.

York said, "He's likely in there waiting for me to come get him. I put him in prison for ten years."

"Good for you!"

As they walked, she told him, teeth chattering, of how Burnham had come to her door with his tale of trying to help a father and son in their buckboard, who'd been attacked by brigands.

"Burnham and his boys," York said, "were

the brigands. They slaughtered those good folk like the many he killed in his raiding days."

Soon they were inside the stable, with its stove-driven warmth and mostly empty stalls, two of which they filled with the gelding and the black Morgan horse.

At the double doors of the barn, as he prepared to leave, Willa said, "What are you going to do, Caleb?"

"I'm going in your house and kill the bastard. If you hear gunshots, one of us will be dead. If it's me, killing him will be up to you."

Many women would have protested this plan, but Willa only nodded, her eyes tight and free of tears. The only expression of her femininity was, after studying him a bit, to kiss him on the mouth before he went out there, a kiss as wet as the outside, but hot, not cold.

Then she said, "You can't die, Caleb York."

"Can't I?"

"No. Then who would be left to make an honest woman out of me?"

He grinned at her and she grinned back, and then he gave her a kiss almost as good as the one she gave him.

Lucas Burnham stormed through the house,

trying to decide where to hide himself to ambush that bastard York. Through a living room window he'd seen that the sheriff of Trinidad had ridden up. Come to the fair damsel's rescue like the damn dime-novel hero fools said he was!

Only the fair damsel had damn near killed Burnham with that rifle, her bullets whistling past him before he shut the door on her. Now he moved quickly through the rooms like a child desperately seeking a hiding place while a playmate covered his eyes and counted to ten ("One Mississippi . . . two Mississippi . . .").

But no place presented itself. The rooms were large, furnished well but sparsely, with wardrobes not closets, and he knew not to hide under a bed, as he remembered shooting right through the mattresses at beds in homes he was raiding and killing those concealing themselves beneath.

Panic set in.

Caleb York was out there, minutes, perhaps seconds away from coming in after him, from confronting the man who had boasted of the vengeance he would take. The man who had mistakenly shot down York's deputy.

Wasn't fair!

Burnham was wounded, and weak from

having to ride in such an unsteady condition. As much as he wanted to take York down, surviving was the important thing now. To live to fight another day . . . unless the opportunity for ambush presented itself. That would serve as well as face to face, because Burnham was a soldier and soldiers did battle — they didn't duel in some mistakenly gentlemanly manner.

So after his brisk, mildly hysterical tour of the Cullen ranch house, Lucas "Burn 'Em" Burnham got into his Rebel jacket — the one he'd taken off a dead Confederate officer years ago — and slung on his gun belt and pulled on his duster and looked for a way the hell out of there.

York went in the unlocked front door, fast and low. He had an immediate view of the long, narrow living room. The only furnishings behind which Burnham might have been hiding were the two big, rough-hewn chairs angled toward the fire, which was really going, flames leaping as if eager to tell York which way the son of a bitch had gone. Staying as near the floor as he could, York approached those chairs, but no one was in or behind them.

The dining room was empty.

And the kitchen.

A study and two bedrooms — no one hiding or plastered to a wall or otherwise lying in wait.

But at the end of the hall that joined all of these rooms, the door to the outside was ajar. York paused before pushing through, listening, but the howl of wind covered any sound his prey might have been making.

So he threw himself out, twisting, to land on his butt in a drift, swinging to face the house. Burnham's best bet would have been to wait with his back against the outside wall and pick York off as he came through.

But Burnham hadn't done that.

Instead, the outlaw was doing something that York considered foolish, even stupid. The sheriff could see his man, running as best he could in the high snow, heading north into the wind, out to where the Cullen spread's pastures yawned invisibly in the eddying snowfall.

York pursued.

Had this been any other outlaw on earth, he might not have met stupidity with stupidity. Might have waited for another day to finish this, as Burnham would surely not let it end here if he could help it. All York had to do was stay put and wait. Wait and watch, looking constantly over his shoulder.

Hell with that.

Yet beneath his woolen scarf, Caleb York was grinning.

Lucas Burnham was scared.

In a spot, the outlaw had reverted to the coward he'd always been, on horseback assaulting unsuspecting civilians, burning down homes and schools and churches and hospitals alongside the guerilla rabble he'd run with, and the captain he so admired who was reviled by North and South alike.

And now the coward was doing another kind of running.

So York pursued.

The stalker with badge and gun could never quite close the distance, though. Fear provided his wounded quarry with fuel. Justice could only keep a lawman going — aided in this case by the depth of wickedness this infamous fugitive bore.

And when Burnham, trudging onward into the wind and sleet and snow, finally began to slow, so did York, who for all his will, remained human. Around them, now that they had drifted through drifts into grazing land blanketed alabaster, horrible sights presented themselves.

Horns of buried cattle stuck out sporadically like the leafless branches of a grotesque dead garden. Here and there little groups of cattle stood in nightmare fashion, this one frozen solid, that one alive but soon to join the others. From another drift rose the seemingly severed head of a dead pony, but as York passed, he could tell that the rest of the animal was there, too, just buried.

How long this went on, York had no idea. He knew only that he would not stop until he had tracked this son of a bitch down. He was well past arresting him. He would rid the world of this malady with a bullet in the head, content in knowing that Lucas Burnham had suffered today out in this frozen desert.

The sky darkening did not become obvious at once because the storm itself was a night of sorts. But the real night had come, all right, and that was when, finally, York lost sight of his prey.

What had become of Burnham, York had no idea. The occasional stray cow — some dead, in various states of blanched burial, others on all fours and waiting for their last roundup — offered the only cover Burnham could have used in a desperate ambush attempt.

But the animals did not provide enough concealment for that. The outlaw had simply angled off in another direction, whether on purpose or accidentally, the wind wiping out any tracks as it had behind the pursuer himself, and now York was alone.

Alone and realizing how much trouble he was in.

The cold, the frostbite, and especially the whistling wind was scoffing at the clothing he thought would protect him. He was far away now, from the Bar-O ranch house grounds. The only sense of where he was, what direction he was going in, was the storm that he'd been pressing through. From the north, it came. So that was north. Straight ahead.

What else was straight ahead?

More snow. More wind. More dead cows.

He staggered up to one such animal, a massive steer, worthy of being called the pride of the Cullen spread. It turned its head just a little, whether to avoid the icy wind or to acknowledge his presence, York couldn't say. His gloved fingers still worked well enough to find, in his coat pocket, the James & Sheffield folding knife. He opened the ivory-handled beauty to its full nine inches, its steel blade etched with a floral design. He slit the steer's throat.

Then York knelt at the fallen animal and, with all his strength, right hand gripping the handle of the knife, the left hand gripping the right, he cut it open from throat till he ran out of anything but tail. An awful avalanche of entrails spilled out.

Then he crawled inside and into a fetal position, the warmth of the dead creature around him as wonderful as the feel of the organs was terrible. Wrapped up in slimy bovine body heat, he risked going to sleep, wondering if he would ever wake.

He woke.

The dead animal and its entrails around him were cold, frozen. They stuck to his clothing some, and snapping sounds — like twigs breaking — accompanied his extrusion from the late beast.

He got to his feet and various sensations coursed through him. Cold, of course. Disgust, from the bits and pieces of cattle innards that stuck to him here and there in various hellish shades, like Joseph's coat of many colors if each hue were horrid. Surprise, or perhaps relief, that he was still alive.

And delight in the absence of snow.

Not that snow wasn't all around. It was everywhere, except in the air.

The downfall had ceased.

The cold hadn't let up. The temperature seemed to have dropped even further. In fact, now as he walked, the snow was frozen over and didn't give way. It was slippery

271

and its feel took a while getting used to, to keep from falling on his ass.

And the wind was still there, the Norther that gave him a hint of where he might be. Only it was halfhearted now. As if Old Man Winter had tired himself out. Given his all. But was keeping up a pathetic front. Still, the Blue Norther came, obviously, from the north. So he walked south. Maybe, with luck — plenty of it — he might find his way back to the Bar-O through this ghastly cemetery of beef, just another stray creature on a vista of frigid death.

Not long after — perhaps fifteen minutes — he came upon a sight he would not soon forget.

Caleb York had finally caught up with Lucas Burnham.

Burnham had propped himself behind a fallen dead steer. The outlaw hadn't climbed into this dead steer, rather used it to sit behind and wait. Wait for Caleb York to come along. Burnham had his Colt in a gloved hand, steadied on the back of the dead animal, as if a target was lined up in his sights.

York laughed.

He laughed loud and hard. Not for long, though, because he lacked the energy. But it was clear that he and Burnham had walked pretty much right past each other after night fell and the storm kept at it. So the outlaw had perched himself here, waiting to finally take his revenge.

Lucas "Burn 'Em" Burnham wouldn't be doing that. "Burn 'Em" Burnham was dead. The icy snow that enveloped him had turned this man, who'd been so proud to wear gray in life, a brilliant blue in death, his face hanging with icicles of various size, his one good eye rolled upward, white touching him everywhere with little brush strokes.

The raider who had burned so many out of their homes and taken so many lives with fire had lost his to an element every bit as deadly.

Which was why Caleb York was smiling even before the little group of riders, led by foreman Earl Colson, found him sliding over, and stumbling through, the snow.

CHAPTER THIRTEEN

In the aftermath of the Big Die-Up, particularly in the northern plains, prairies were piled with decomposing cattle.

Cows aborted calves that would otherwise have boosted herds, and those dogies that did survive were the meat of coyotes and wolves, who, like many a Western outlaw, faced a bounty (twenty dollars per wolf pelt, a buck fifty for a coyote). Meanwhile, starving herds with no cud to chew settled for tar paper from ranch house walls, bark from cotton-woods, and wool from decaying sheep remains.

Many ranchers reacted to the disaster by quitting, one Montana cattle baron saying, "A business that had been fascinating to me before became distasteful," adding that he never again wanted to own an animal that he couldn't feed and shelter.

Bones of cattle were rounded up and sold back east for fertilizer, the scent of prairie flow-

ers overwhelmed by the odor of death. Rotting beef choked rivers and creeks to where water was no longer safe to drink. And some skeletons of cattle and horses would continue to be discovered in gullies and pastures over the next twenty years.

Trinidad, and most of the New Mexico Territory, however, fared better than most.

The big ceramic thermometer on the wall outside Harris Mercantile said 60 degrees Fahrenheit. Three days before it had read 3 degrees below zero. Only vague hints of the snow and ice that had shrouded Trinidad remained, and the more typical New Mexico winter weather dried everything out almost overnight.

The only exception was Main Street — not the buildings, but the thoroughfare that regularly wore sand carted in from the nearby Purgatory River to hold the dust down. That sand was a virtual riverbed itself now, a sloppy, soppy mess. Patrons were walking into shops and leaving sandy footprints behind. The same brooms that had tried, often vainly, to clear snow from the boardwalk into the street were now sweeping sand from the floors of the shops onto the boardwalk and back out into the street.

Caleb York — now wearing a shorter, hip-length black frock coat (his longer one finally at the seamstress), his pearl-buttoned gray shirt, a black string tie, and his tied-down holstered .44 — walked the boardwalk in late morning, happy to see town folk out in the sunshine. Ladies promenaded in bonnets and gingham, some joined by men in derbies and cutaway jackets that showed off their vests and watch chains. The citizens were all smiles, the blizzard of '87 already fading into memory and anecdote.

York showed few physical signs of what he'd endured, just some tender pink flesh around his temples. He had been brought in off the wintry pasture by the Bar-O foreman and his riders, and set on one of several horses they'd recovered. He had been delivered to the ranch house, where a tub of warm water was prepared by Willa. Someone — he had no memory of any of that — had helped him into the water and washed him gently with scented soap.

Must have been Willa, a thought that didn't embarrass him really, now that they'd shared a bed.

She was also likely the one who'd got him into one of her father's nightshirts and guided him to George Cullen's bed, where he slept around the clock. He'd woken in the late morning two days after his pursuit of Burnham into the cold. The covers were pulled back and Dr. Miller was examining him.

York asked, "Will I lose any ears or fingers or my nose, Doc?"

Miller, apparently finished with his inspection, flipped the covers back in place, pulled a chair up bedside, pointlessly smoothed his rumpled brown suit coat, and sat.

"Nothing wrong that I can see," the doctor said, "except exhaustion, to which you've been applying Nature's remedy yourself."

York propped himself on a pillow. "Sleep, you mean."

The plump little bespectacled physician nodded. "You must have bundled yourself up good. You suffered a touch of first-degree frostbite around the eyes, but otherwise seems you covered up. I hear you crawled into a cow."

It did burn around his eyes some. Nodding, he said, "Turnabout's fair play. After all, I put enough beef in my belly, over time."

That mildly amused the doc, which York figured was about all the remark deserved.

"Some aren't so lucky," Miller said. "Some lost a foot or two. And not everybody in Trinidad has ten fingers and toes now. But

277

for the most part, folks got themselves inside and stayed warm."

"And have you restored Tulley to his sickbed?"

The doc's smile was wry. "No, your deputy's a stubborn old fool. He's returned to watch the jailhouse office till you get back. I made him promise to take it easy. No rounds, just hold things down. I, uh, have restored the sickroom. Got the blood off the floor, bleached the stain out. Would hate to give future patients the wrong idea."

York frowned. "Do you know if Burnham's body has been recovered?"

Miller nodded. "Apparently you were insistent about that when they brought you in. That foreman had some men collect him. Mr. Burnham is wrapped up in my buckboard outside right now, like a late Christmas present."

"Good," York said with a tight smile. "Deliver him to the undertaker's. Tell Perkins he's welcome to thaw the bastard out and put him in the window."

"With a sign that says 'Tracked and killed by Caleb York'?"

"I didn't kill him. God and Mother Nature conspired on his doom. 'Tracked down by' would do it. Get the newspaper man, Penniman, to have a picture of the deceased

278

taken. In the window or out, I don't care."

Miller frowned. "What the hell for, Caleb?"

"Proof. That son of a bitch is worth five hundred dollars dead or alive. A sheriff has to make an honest living."

The doc nodded, having no argument with that thinking.

"If Perkins hasn't already buried them," York went on, "have Penniman get photographs of the other three deceased outlaws, too. They may be worth something, dead, too. Lord knows they weren't worth much alive."

"They're in the undertaker's window already," he said. "Likely getting ripe." The doctor gathered his Gladstone bag, rose, and said, "Get some more rest, Caleb. You don't need any other medication than that."

The doctor went out, and soon York had taken the medic's advice, falling back into slumber. He woke with darkness at the windows and Willa Cullen at his bedside.

The seated young woman wore a green-and-black plaid shirt and Levi's, typical for this daughter of a rancher. But now she *was* the rancher, wasn't she? She had her folded hands in her lap and her cornflower-blue eyes were on him as he stirred. Despite her tomboy apparel, she was quite lovely, her blond hair pinned atop her head in circling braids, somehow suggesting a Viking woman.

He asked, "How long have I been here?"

"A full day and night," she said, "and all of today until now. You should stay put."

"Have I been out of this bed?"

"No."

"I'd like to be. Are my clothes dry?"

Willa nodded, but added, "The doctor brought you some clean things." She gestured to a dresser, where the clothing was stacked neatly on top. "Would you like to get into them?"

"Yes."

She rose. "I'll leave you to it then."

He got into the clothes, then found her at the kitchen table with a cup of coffee before her and another cup waiting for him. He told her he needed the privy and she asked if he needed help getting out there.

"No," he said. "I'm fine."

In truth he was somewhat unsteady, but he made the round trip, almost startled by the warming change of temperature, and joined her again at the table.

He sipped the hot black coffee, then said, "I'm so relieved that bastard didn't hurt you. He *didn't,* did he?"

"No. As I said, he was playing a role. A

'distressed wayfarer.' "

"Kind of you to . . . house me."

"Don't be silly." She seemed to have something on her mind, holding the cup of coffee in both her hands, warming them. She stared into the liquid as if it bore answers to questions unasked. "Caleb . . ."

"Yes, Willa?"

Emotionlessly, she said, "I want you to know . . . what happened between us . . . I mean to exert no hold on you. We both of us knew what we were doing. Acted of our own free will. You are not beholden to me for . . . for what I willingly shared."

Her eyes were not on him, but his were very much on her.

Then, in an almost accusatory manner, York asked, "Do you love me?"

She looked up sharply, as stunned as if he'd slapped her. "What kind of question is that to ask?"

"The right one. Well, I love *you,* woman, so let's hear where you stand."

She swallowed, eyes aimed into her coffee again. "I know what it means to be able to live a life you've chosen. I was raised to this one, and all its hardships . . . and there are plenty of those right now. But it's the life I want. I raise cattle. You hunt men. I would not ask you to raise beef any more than you would ask me to wear a badge."

He smiled a little.

"Don't laugh at me, Caleb York."

"I'm not laughing. I was just picturing you dressed like Jonathan P. Tulley, though a badge on *your* chest would hang different."

Now she smiled, then didn't. "You know what I'm saying to you. Neither of us should expect the other to change their way of life. I don't know that either of us could."

They sat there saying nothing for a while.

He sipped coffee. "Temperature's come up considerable, out there. Thaw is setting in."

"It is."

"How hard hit is the Bar-O?"

"Too early to say. Three men gone, found next to their frozen ponies. The herd down by a third, at least. My foreman tells me he came upon thousands of beeves bunched against fencing. He snipped the fences to let them roam and maybe find shelter, but . . . but some were so bad off, their skin split open and their hoofs dropped off. Dozens of young steers drifted on stumps, tails cracked like broken branches. In one spot, the bodies got stacked up so high, latecomers could scale over them, just to head deeper into white death. The moans of suffering cattle . . . . Colson said he'd seen plenty as a soldier, but nothing the like of this. He said it would melt the heart of a man colder than the storm itself."

She covered her face with one hand, then both. He got up and bent beside her, slipping an arm around her.

"I'm sorry," she said.

"Nothing to apologize for," he said. "Even a strong woman cries. Men too, sometimes."

She lowered her hands and looked at him, her face streaked with tears, her sorrow not quite defeating her beauty. "How can I ask you to be part of this, Caleb? The Bar-O may not even exist a year from now."

"You don't need me to run the Bar-O."

She swallowed.

"We'll find some other way," he said. "I can give you comfort and loyalty. You can hire men who know the cattle business. You don't need one for your husband. For that all you need is a man who understands and loves you."

Her eyes narrowed, the cornflowers floating in a red setting. "*That's* what you would be to me? Husband?"

"If you'll have me."

"How . . . how would it work?"

"We'll figure that out."

York stood, let out a breath, and stretched his arms high.

283

"Do you think I'm fit to head back to town?" he asked. "Or do I need another night's rest here?"

She reached out and took his hand. "Another night's rest, for certain. But those covers of yours . . . they're anything but fresh. Let's see if there's another bed around here you might get into."

She found one.

Now York was in Trinidad, strolling the boardwalk. Town folk greeted him and, seeing him coming or going, talked about him admiringly. The legend called Caleb York was back in town, tipping his hat to them. If they only knew how tired he felt, and how patches of skin on his face near his eyes burned from the frostbite.

He'd already checked in with his deputy, who he found seated at the jailhouse desk, as if Tulley were the sheriff. The old desert rat had scurried from behind there and settled back at his beat-up table near the potbellied stove, which was lit only enough to provide heat for the liquid the deputy insisted was coffee.

"Caleb York," Jonathan P. Tulley said, "the winder at the undertaker's is just cram full of dead men you made. Ye should be proud."

"I'll be proud for the bounties to come in," the sheriff said. "I'll give you whatever

Warlow brings, and split Fender with you."

"Sounds right fair! Looks like I'll have me some *real* money, won't I? Buy me some more of them proper clothes, fit for a deputy." His eyes narrowed. "Tell me, Sheriff — is it true what they be sayin'?"

"What are they saying?"

"That ye knocked out the biggest steer on the Bar-O with one dang punch, cut him from his throat to his stud works, then crawled inside and took a nice winter's nap . . . ?"

"Not true."

"No?"

"Had to punch him twice."

Tulley thought about that, then went "hee-hee" with laughter.

York got up, put on his hat, and started out the door, saying, as he so often did to the deputy, "Hold down the fort."

"Where ye be off to?"

"Victory. Like to see how Miss Filley made out during the blizzard."

"I bet ye would!" Tulley cackled. "I bet ye would!"

Soon York was seated at a table in the Victory. The saloon, doing modest business, was serving its free lunch. The sheriff helped himself to sandwich makings — corned beef, yellow cheese, and rye bread, plus some smoked herring and a dill pickle.

He had just finished the sandwich when Rita Filley appeared and sat beside him, delivering a glass of beer. She wore a green satin gown — even midday, she played her role to the hilt, her spilling décolletage a further inducement for male clientele.

She said with a lilt in her voice, "I see you're still alive."

He nodded, sipped the beer. "I see you're no longer maintainin' a hotel for stray cowhands."

"No, all my little strays have wandered back to their ranches."

"Probably in no hurry. Those boys do not have pleasant duty ahead."

She frowned, shuddered a little. "So I've heard. I also hear you had quite the time filling the undertaker's window so vividly. Some wild stories going around."

"Like the one where I rode a wild bucking bronco to death, then bit him open stem to stern and slithered inside to get some rest?"

"I heard a version of that. I think it's only going to get better."

"Depends on what you consider 'better.' " He gave her as warm a smile as he dared. "I wanted to tell you how much I admire what you did for those stranded cowboys. Housing, feeding them. If you want to tally up your expenses, I'll take them to the Citizens Committee."

She shook her head. "No thanks. Even a saloon owner has to pitch in her civic duty sometimes."

"You're a good man, woman." He wiped his face with a napkin, pushed his empty plate away, finished the beer, then said, "Listen. Something you need to know."

Her expression would have been unreadable, had her eyes not tightened a touch. "All right. I'm always ready to be better informed."

"I, uh . . . things have turned serious with Miss Cullen and myself."

She swallowed, twitched a smile, nodded. "I'm not surprised. I've noticed you're fond of her."

"By serious, I mean . . ."

"I know what you mean."

His mouth smiled but his forehead frowned. "It's just . . . Rita, I think the world of you. I don't know that there's anyone's friendship I value more."

She drew a breath. Let it out. Said, "Wonderful to hear."

"I'm not a perfect man."

"No, really?"

He smiled, shrugged. "I just mean . . . I have no intention of taking advantage of you. We need to keep this friendly, but, uh . . ."

"You won't be going upstairs with me anymore."

He said nothing for a while.

Then, quietly: "No."

"Understood," she said.

He gestured helplessly. "Could you respect a man who went back and forth between two women? Who played it fast and loose in such a way?"

"Of course not." She smiled and there was warmth in it. Reached out and touched his hand. Warmth in that, too. "Don't give it another thought."

She squeezed his hand and took hers away. "You know what they say," she said, with a painted smile. " 'Woman's work is never done.' " She and her smile rose. "Have to get to the bookkeeping, I'm afraid."

And she went up the stairs.

Alone.

What she did up there, however, was not bookkeeping. And while the possibility did not occur to him, Rita was making the very point York had made to Willa, earlier.

Even a strong woman can cry.

A TIP OF THE STETSON

The very real blizzard that became known as the Big Die-Up (aka the Great Die-Up) serves as the historical backdrop of this novel. My approach to the Caleb York novels, however, is not generally that of the historical novelist.

I admit feeling a certain push/pull, because in my historical mystery and crime novels — in particular the Nathan Heller series — I often look at real mysteries and crimes, dropping a traditional private detective in the Philip Marlowe/Mike Hammer mode into an extensively researched examination of the subject at hand.

But in following the late Mickey Spillane's lead, established in his various film script drafts and notes about the York character and his world, I have been more concerned with the mythic West than the real one.

The first book in the series, *The Legend of Caleb York* (2015), based on Mickey's unproduced screenplay, clearly establishes an approach in the Hollywood tradition. Which is fine with me, as I grew up on John Wayne, Randolph Scott, Joel McCrea, and Audie Murphy movies, as well as American television's Western craze of the late fifties, with the Warner Bros. series *Maverick* a personal favorite.

My desire is to present the mythic West in a framework of the real one, to provide authentic underpinnings to my fanciful tales, much as a noir detective novel indulges in melodrama set against a gritty reality. This of course means that I am beholden to research, and while I am sure I have overlooked some of my sources, I wish at least to acknowledge the ones that were most helpful.

I would not be surprised to find that every one of my contemporaries in the Western fiction field uses the following two books: *The Writer's Guide to Everyday Life in the Wild West from 1840–1900* (1999), Candy Moulton; and *Everyday Life in the 1800s: A Guide for Writers, Students, and Historians* (1993), Marc McCutcheon. Of the numerous books on firearms in my library, I chiefly use *Guns of the American West* (2009), Dennis Adler. The previous novels in this series all drew upon these invaluable sources.

For this novel in particular, with its emphasis on the blizzard of 1886 to 1887, I consulted *Cattle Kingdom: The Hidden History of the Cowboy West* (2017), Christopher Knowlton; *Cowboys, Ranching & Cattle Trails: A New Mexico Federal Writers' Project Book* (2013), compiled and edited by Ann Lacy and Anne Valley-Fox; *Cowboys: The Real Story of Cowboys and Cattlemen* (1974), Royal B. Hassrick; *Frontier Stories: A New Mexico Federal Writers' Project Book* (2010), compiled and edited by Ann Lacy and Anne Valley-Fox; *The Real Wild West: The 101 Ranch and the Creation of the American West* (1999), Michael Wallis; and *Winning the Wild West: The Epic Saga of the American Frontier 1800–1899* (2002), Page Stegner.

I often wonder how I was able to write historical novels prior to Internet search engines, and yet most of the Nathan Heller novels and all of the Eliot Ness ones were written strictly using old-fashioned methods, such as newspaper, magazine, and book research, requiring countless trips to the local library and used bookstores. Now — as I imagine is the case for most writers of fiction working today but setting their stories in the past — I am able to do a lot of it on the fly. What did a hardware store look like in the 1880s? What brand names of whiskey were around? When was the snow globe invented? And on and on.

I will not include Web addresses, as those change and disappear from time to time, and will instead provide article names and authors (and sometimes Web sites), which Google and other search engines should find for you.

The following material directly relates to the Blizzard of 1886 to 1887: "The 1887 Blizzard That Changed the American Frontier Forever," Laura Clark, *Smithsonian;* "The Great Die-Up," Mark Boardman, *Inside History;* "The Blizzard of 1886: When the West Froze," *Ancestral Findings;* "The Big Die-Up: The Death of the Old West," Ron Soodalter, *American Cowboy;* "The Great Die Up," M. Timothy Nolting, *The Fence Post;* and "The Winter That Changed Cattle Ranching Forever," Caroline Clemmons, *Sweethearts of the West.*

I looked at half a dozen articles on bank robberies in the Old West, none better than "The Non-Existent Frontier Bank Robbery," (if a somewhat overstated thesis) by Larry Schweikert, at the *Foundation of Economic Education* site. For saddle shop information I drew upon "Saddlemakers of the Old West," Raymond L. Ledesma, at the *Western Saddle Guide* site, and "Silver & Saddles," Jennifer Denison, *Western Horseman* magazine's site.

Of a number of articles online that I utilized for the characterization of Lucas Burnham, perhaps the most helpful was "William Quantrill — Renegade Leader of the Missouri Border War," Kathy Weiser, *Legends of America* site. Not every history buff agrees with the negative portrayal in this article and elsewhere of Quantrill. That same site includes an interesting positive view of the notorious raider, by Paul R. Petersen, "William Quantrill — The Man, the Myth, the Soldier." My apologies to Quantrill fans, and remind them that the fictional Burnham is the villain here, not his captain.

Also at the excellent *Legends of America* site is "Las Vegas, New Mexico — As Wicked as Dodge City," Kathy Weiser. Also helpful was "Getting Lost in History in the Other Las Vegas," Steven Talbot, *The New York Times.*

My thanks to the authors of these books and articles. Also, thank you to my supportive editor, Michaela Hamilton; my agent and friend, Dominick Abel; and my wife (and in-house editor), Barbara Collins.

ABOUT THE AUTHORS

Mickey Spillane is the legendary crime writer who created Mike Hammer (*I, the Jury; Kiss Me Deadly*). Before his death at the age of 88 in 2006, Spillane chose long-time friend Max Allan Collins to complete his unfinished works and act as his literary executor.

Max Allan Collins, a Mystery Writers of America Grand Master, is a bestselling author of fiction, nonfiction, and graphic novels, including *Road to Perdition,* adapted into the Tom Hanks film, and *Quarry,* basis of a Cinemax series. He lives in Iowa and can be found online at www.MaxAllan Collins.com.

The employees of Thorndike Press hope you have enjoyed this Large Print book. All our Thorndike, Wheeler, and Kennebec Large Print titles are designed for easy reading, and all our books are made to last. Other Thorndike Press Large Print books are available at your library, through selected bookstores, or directly from us.

For information about titles, please call:
(800) 223-1244

or visit our website at:
gale.com/thorndike

To share your comments, please write:
Publisher
Thorndike Press
10 Water St., Suite 310
Waterville, ME 04901